CA   Y
LI   W9-ANV-335

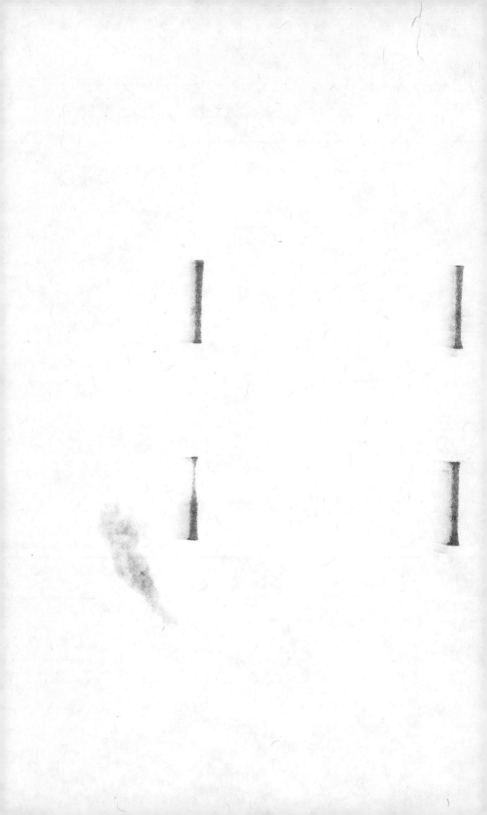

SEARCHING FOR SURVIVORS

BOOKS BY RUSSELL BANKS

Waiting To Freeze (poetry)
Snow (poetry)
Family Life (novel)

Searching for
Survivors

RUSSELL BANKS

FICTION COLLECTIVE NEW YORK 1975

CARL A. RUDISILL LIBRARY
LENOIR RHYNE COLLEGE

Many of these stories first appeared in periodicals: "The Neighbor" and "Searching for Survivors (I)" in *Fiction*; "The Defenseman" in *Fire Exit*; "With Che in New Hampshire" and "The Drive Home" in *New American Review*; "The Masquerade" in *New Story*; "The Blizzard" and "The Investiture" in *Partisan Review*; "With Che at The Plaza" in *Plowshares*; "With Che at Kitty Hawk" in *Shendoah*. "With Che in New Hampshire" was also published in the anthology, *Best American Short Stories* 1971, and "With Che at Kitty Hawk" was one of the *O. Henry Prize Stories for 1974.*

All the characters in this book are fictitious, and any resemblance to actual persons, living or dead, is purely coincidental.

813.54
B22s
96646
Mar 1976

This publication is in part made possible with support from the New York State Council on the Arts

First Edition

Copyright © 1975 by Russell Banks
All rights reserved
Typesetting by
New Hampshire Composition
Library of Congress Catalog No. 74 - 24911
ISBN: 0 - 914590 - 06 - 5 (paperback)
ISBN: 0 - 914590 - 07 - 3 (hardcover)

Published by **FICTION COLLECTIVE**

Distributed by *George Braziller, Inc.*
One Park Avenue
New York, N. Y. 10016

to Christopher Banks — in memory

CONTENTS

"What would we poor people do, if we could not always come up with some idea, like country, love, art and religion, with which we can again and again cover up that dark black hole. This limitless solitude in eternity. Being alone."

—Max Beckmann, **Briefe im Kriege**, p. 66, letter of 5/24/1915.

SEARCHING FOR SURVIVORS (I)

Poor Henry Hudson, I miss him. It's almost as if I had been aboard the leaking *Discovery* myself, a cabin boy or maybe an ordinary seaman, and had been forced to decide, Which will it be, slip into line behind the callow mutineers and get the hell out of this closing, ice-booming bay and home again to dear, wet England? Or say nay and climb over the side behind the good Commodore, the gentle, overthrown master of the *Discovery*, settling down next to him in the open shallop, the slate-grey, ice-flecked water lurking barely six inches below the gunwales of the overloaded rowboat, as the ship puts on sail, catches a safe slice of wind rising out of the Arctic and drives for open seas, east and south. . . .

I would've had no choice—assuming I was given one. I would have stuck with the bigger boat and would have watched the smaller one, Hudson standing darkly iron-willed in the low bow, as it gradually became a black speck on the sheet of white-rimmed lead behind us, and then disappeared altogether.

It's so easy to forget him, to let my memory of him gradually disappear, the way his image, for one who stood at the stern of the *Discovery*, disappeared. 1611, after all, is a long ways back. Which is why I'm truly grateful whenever I happen to be reminded of him and his loss, and mine—when driving over the Hudson River, say, the fiery red sun setting behind grey New Jersey marshes, or when driving the curly length of the Henry Hudson Parkway north of Manhattan. (Though I've never been to Hudson Bay, I believe that some-day I will go there for a season.)

Oddly, reminded of Hudson, I'm always reminded in turn of other things. Mainly automobiles. The automobiles of my

adolescence, for some reason. There are doubtless deep asso-
ciations. Whenever I happen to have ended a dark day by suddenly, accidentally, conjuring bright images of Henry Hudson
lost in the encroaching white silence of his bay, I usually
remember the first car I ever owned. It was the unadorned
frame of a 1929 Model A Ford. I was fifteen, not old enough
to take it out on the road legally, but that was all right
because I intended to spend the next two years building it
into a hot rod. Hot rods were very important to almost everyone, one way or another, in the late fifties. My closest friend
Daryl, who was sixteen, was building his hot rod out of a
1940 Ford coupe that was up on cinderblocks behind his
father's garage. He already had an engine for it, a '53 Chrysler overhead valve V-8 which lay on its side inside the garage,
in front of his father's car. That car was an impeccable 1949
Hudson Hornet, which my friend Daryl, whenever his father
felt reckless enough to concede it, was old enough to drive.
This happened rarely, because the Hudson was Daryl's
father's obsession. A tense, thin man, short and drawn in on
himself like a hair-triggered crossbow. I remember him as
always rubbing gently the sleek skin of that car with a clean,
soft cloth in the speckled-orange, autumn sunlight of a Saturday afternoon, the slow circles of the cloth seeming to tran-
quilize the grim man as he worked.

No other single experience with a machine compared to
the exquisitely abstracted yet purely sensual pleasure provided by Daryl's father's Hudson. Riding in that car, sunk
deeply into the drugging hug of the back seat, was to me,
then, like relaxing after having won an unprovoked fistfight
with a tattooed pipe fitter in a tavern that served minors.
Which of course never happened. Bars like that, where one
could perform heroically, were only rumored to exist.

Almost a decade old, the Hudson still enjoyed precisely
the condition it had relished the day Daryl's father had purchased it, in 1949, March, at the Hudson assembly plant in
Michigan, after having followed it step by step down the
entire length of the assembly line, watching it magically becoming itself, until it was emptied out the dark mouth of the
factory into the shattering sunlight of the test track. Then,
with meticulously organized pleasure, he had driven it all the
way home to Wakefield, Massachusetts.

The car was deep green, the color of oak leaves in July, and the restrained stabs of chrome on the grill and bumpers and around the headlights and taillights merely deepened the sense of well-being that one took from such huge expanses of color. Shaped more or less like an Indian burial mound from the Upper Mississippi Valley, whether stilled or in motion, the vehicle expressed permanence and stability, blocky, arrogant pacts with eternity.

Later on, when I was nineteen, I was foot-loose and almost broke, and needing transportation from central Florida out to the West Coast, I bought a breaking-down 1947 Studebaker for fifteen dollars, and it got me as far as Amarillo, Texas, where it wheezingly expired. Then for a long time I didn't own a car. I hitchhiked or used public transportation or rode around passively in friends' cars—lost touch completely with the needs of an earlier aesthetic.

Then, a few years after the Studebaker and Texas, when I was about twenty-three, I guess, I happened to be living in Boston, working as a timekeeper on a construction job at the Charlestown Navy Yard, and one silver-frosted morning in February, I walked sleepily out of the MTA station and headed down the brick sidewalk towards the drydocked *U.S.S. Constitution* and the derrick-cluttered Navy Yard beyond and nearly collided with my old friend Daryl. He was dressed in an expensive-looking charcoal grey, pinstriped suit with a vest and a black wool overcoat with a silver fur collar. He wore a derby, a black bowler, perched atop his bony head, and he was clenching a black, tightly furled umbrella.

Daryl! I shouted. I hadn't seen him in five or six years at least. How the hell *are* you!

He responded politely, but with painful reserve, obviously eager to get away from me. He was working on State Street, he told me (when I asked), aiming to be a broker, taking night courses in business administration, living in a flat here in Charlestown in the interim. I asked him about his family, of course, as a matter of simple courtesy, but also because I really had liked and respected his father, that grimly organized sensualist. Daryl told me that his father, a foreman at the Wonder Bread factory in Somerville, had retired two

years ago and then had died, six months later, of a heart
attack. His mother, always an invisible person to me anyhow, now lived alone in a condominium in Maryland.

We shook hands and exchanged addresses and promised
to get in touch as soon as possible, so we could really sit
down and have a talk. Then we rushed off in our opposite
directions.

I strode quickly through the gate to the Yard and jogged
past warehouses towards the new steam plant, and for a
second I thought I felt lonelier than I'd ever felt before. I
knew that nowadays loneliness was probably the last thing
old Daryl was troubled by. First things first.

I pictured his small blue eyes darting past my own as they
sought a spot in space over my shoulder and about twelve
feet behind me, where they could rest easy while Daryl and
I talked to each other. No way to deny it: I truly had expected him to become a successful racing driver. Or at least
a well-known mechanic.

I live in the country now, in central New Hampshire, and
two months ago I answered an ad in the local newspaper and
bought a Norwegian elkhound puppy, a male, a grey puff of
fur with a pointed black face and curl of a tail. I named him
Hudson, giving him the second name of Frobisher, so I could
be sure I was naming him after the explorers of the Arctic
seas—appropriate for a dog of that explicit a breeding.

It's occurred to me lately that in a few years, if I want
to, I can put together a team of these rugged Arctic dogs,
and I can race them in nearby Laconia, where the annual
National Sled Dog Championship Races are held. The prize
money isn't much, but it's said that great satisfaction derives
from handling a team of dogs under such strenuous circumstances. There's a regular race course, and you're supposed
to end up back where you started, on Main Street in Laconia,
after a couple hours of following red triangular flags
through the surrounding countryside. I know that I would
pull off the course after a while, never finishing the race. I'd
just light out for the back country, where you can drive all
day on top of ten feet of snow and ice. Imagine driving a
dozen half-wild, Norwegian elkhound sled dogs into billow-

ing sheets of snow, leaving the settlement and swiftly disappearing behind the dogs into timeless, silent whiteness.

When spring came, I'd be circling the muddied edge of Hudson Bay on foot, looking at the wet ground for pieces of old iron or charred wood, or maybe a yellowed, half-rotted journal—signs that Hudson had made it to shore. If he made it that far, the Cree or the Esquimaux would have helped him, and he would have survived there peacefully into old age, telling and retelling to the few of us who'd elected to leave the *Discovery* with him the amazing tales of earlier voyages.

There was the 1607 attempt for the Moscovy Company to cut across the Arctic, north from Norway all the way to 80° latitude at Hakluyt's Headland on Spitzbergen, before fields of ice finally stopped him.

There was the second voyage for the Muscovy, in 1608, eastward around the top of Russia, until he was blocked by ice, headlands, and headwinds.

There was the 1609 voyage, for the Dutch East India Company. This time, headed northeast around Russia again, mutiny stopped him, and he turned back.

Then there was the year, 1610, financed by a group of Englishmen, that Hudson and his entire crew in the *Discovery* lay icebound in his bay atop the North American continent.

After the second and final mutiny, there was the year it took for Hudson and his three loyal sailors to cross the bay to the western shore, dragging the shallop filled with their dwindling supplies all the way across the endless, silent ice pack.

WITH CHE IN NEW HAMPSHIRE

So here I am, still wandering. All over the face of the earth. Mexico, Central America, South America. Then Africa. Working my way north to the Mediterranean, resting for a season in the Balearic Islands. Then Iberia, all of Gaul, the British Isles. Scandinavia. Then I show up in the Near East, disappearing as suddenly and unexpectedly as I appeared. Reappearing in Moscow. Before I can be interviewed, I have dropped out of sight again, showing up farther east, photographed laughing with political prisoners outside Vladivostok, getting into a taxi in Kyoto, lying on a beach near Melbourne, drinking in a nightclub in Honolulu (a club known for its underworld clientele). Chatting amiably with Indians in Peru. And then I drop out of sight altogether. . . .

All this from the file they have on me in Washington. They know that somehow I am dangerous to them, but they are unable to determine in what way I am dangerous, for everything is rumor and suspicion, and I am never seen except when alone or in the cheerful company of harmless peasant-types. My finances are easily explained: I have none. I never own anything that I can't carry with me and can't leave out in the rain, and I am a hitchhiker wherever I go. I accept no money whatsoever from outside sources that might be considered suspicious. Occasionally I find employ-ment for a few weeks at some menial job—as a dockhand in Vera Cruz, a truckdriver in North Africa, a construction worker in Turkey—and occasionally I accept lavish gifts from American women traveling to forget their wrecked lives at home.

Okay, so here I am again, wandering, and everything is different, except that I am alone. Everything else is different.

And then one day, late in spring, I turn up in Crawford, New Hampshire. Home. Alone, as usual. I'm about thirty-five, say. No older. A lot has happened to me in the interim: when I step down from the Boston-to-Montreal bus at Mc-Allister's General Store, I am walking with an evident limp. My left leg, say, doesn't bend at the knee. Everything I own is in the duffle bag I carry, and I own nothing that cannot be left out in the rain. I want it that way. . . .

Rerun my getting off the bus. The cumbersome Greyhound turns slowly off Route 28 just north of Pittsfield, where the small, hand-lettered sign points CRAWFORD 1/2 MI., and then rumbles down into the heart of the valley, past the half-dozen, century-old, decaying houses, past Conway's ESSO station to McAllister's Gulf station and general store, where the bus driver applies the air brakes to his vehicle, which has been coasting since it turned off Route 28, and it hisses to a stop.

The door pops open in front of me, and I pitch my duffle down to the ground and then ease my pain-wracked body down the steps and out the door to where my duffle has landed on the ground. . . .

A few old men and Bob McAllister. . . . A few old men and Bob McAllister, like turtles, sit in the late-morning sun on the roofless front porch that runs the width of the store building. Two of the old men, one on each side of the screen door, are seated on straight-backed, soda-fountain chairs, which they lean back against the wall. One old man is squatting and scratches on the board floor with a pen-knife. The others (for there should be more than three) are arrayed in various postures across the porch.

Even though the sun feels warm against my skin, the air is cool, reminding me of the winter that has just ended, the dirty remnants of snow in shady corners between buildings, snow that melted, finally, just last week, and the mushy dirt roads that are beginning to dry out at last. The old men seated on the stagelike platform in front of me stare down at me without embarrassment. This is because they don't recognize me. Through the glass behind their heads I can see the semidarkness of the interior of the store and the shape of

Alma McAllister's perpetually counting head. She is stationed
at the check-out counter, which is actually a kitchen table.
Beyond her, I can pick out the shapes of three or four parallel
rows of canned foods, the meat locker, and the large refrigera-
tion unit that holds all of McAllister's dairy products, his
frozen foods, packaged bacon and sausage, eggs, cold drinks,
and beer. And farther back in the store, I can make out the
dim shapes of hoses, buckets, garden tools, work clothes,
fishing rods, and the other miscellaneous items that finish
out the store's inventory—Bob McAllister's wild guess at the
material needs of his neighbors.

The old men staring at me. They are wondering who the
hell I might be. They don't recognize me at all, not yet anyway, although I was able to recognize them as soon as I could
see their faces. It is I who have changed, not they, and I have
thought of them many times in the last few years, whereas
they probably have not once thought of me.

Bob McAllister, of course, is there. And old Henry Davis,
he would have to be there too. His sister died back in 1967,
I recall as soon as I see his sun-browned, leathery face, remembering that I learned of the event from a letter my
mother wrote to me while I was in Florida waiting to hear
from Ché.

The others, now. There is John Alden, who claims he is
a direct descendant of the original John and Priscilla Alden.
He is. Gaunt, white-maned and silent, except to speak of the
time, and always dressed in a black suit, tobacco-stained
white shirt, and black necktie, and continually drawing from
his pocket the large gold watch that the Boston & Maine
Railroad gave him when he retired, back in 1962, drawing it
out and checking its time against anybody else's—the radio's,
the church's, Bob McAllister's, Timex's, anybody's who
happens to walk into the store.

"What time you got, Henry?"

"I got ten-seventeen, John."

"Check it again, Henry, 'cause I got ten-twenty one."

"Thanks, John, thanks a lot. Hell of a watch you got
there. It ain't ever wrong, is it?"

"Not yet it ain't. Not yet."

There are two or three others. There is Bob McAllister,

who comes over to the bus as he has done every day for over twenty years and takes the bundle of Boston newspapers from the driver. There is Henry Davis, who plowed the few acres that my father cultivated every year with corn and potatoes and the meadows that were hayed when I was a child—but that was before Henry and his horses got too old and Pa had to go to Concord and buy a Ford tractor to replace Henry. And there is John Alden, who is a direct descendant of John and Priscilla. And there would be Dr. Cotton, too, because it's about five years from now, and Dr. Cotton has retired, no doubt, has left his entire practice to that young Dr. Annis from Laconia, the new fellow from Laconia my mother told me about in her letters. . . .

That's four, which is enough. They don't recognize me. Although when Bob McAllister lifts himself off the porch and crosses between the Gulf gasoline pumps to the bus to receive the Boston papers, he stares at me quizzically as he passes, seeming to think that he knows me from someplace and time, but he can't remember from where or when, so he merely nods, for courtesy's sake as well as safety's, and strolls by.

I bend down and pick up my duffle, heave it easily to my right shoulder—three years in the jungles of Guatemala have left me with one leg crippled and deep scars on my face and mind forever. But the years have also toughened me, and my arms and back are as hard as rock maple.

Close-up of the scar on my face. It starts, thin and white, like a scrap of white twine, high up on my left temple, and then runs jaggedly down to my cheekbone, where it broadens and jigs suddenly back and down, eventually disappearing below my earlobe. Naturally, I am reluctant to talk about how it happened, but anyone who cares to can see that it is the result of a machete blow, and the fact that I am alive at all— however scarred— is a clear indication of what happened to the man with the machete.

The driver closes the door to his bus and releases the air brakes hurriedly, for he is no doubt relieved to be rid of a passenger whose silent intensity had somehow unnerved him from the moment he left the Park Square Greyhound Bus

Terminal in Boston until the moment when the man, without saying a word to anyone, not even to the fat Canadian
sitting next to him, finally rose from his seat, which was
immediately behind the driver, and stepped down in Crawford. The driver closes the door to his bus, releases the air
brakes hurriedly, and the big, slab-sided, silver vehicle pulls
away, heads back to Route 28 for Alton Bay and Laconia,
and then north to Montreal. . . .

The cool, dry air feels wonderful against my face. It's been
too long. I've been away from this comforting, life-giving air
too long this time. I had forgotten its clarity, the way it
handles the light—gently, but with crispness and efficiency.
I had forgotten the way a man, if he can get himself up high
enough, can see through the air that fills the valley between
him and a single tree or chimney or gable which is actually
miles away from him, making the man feel like a hawk
floating thousands of feet above the earth's surface, looping
lazily in a cloudless sky, hour after hour, while tiny creatures
huddle in warm, dark niches below and wait in terror for him
to grow weary of the hunt and drift away. . . .

Leaving Mexico City. As I boarded the Miami-bound jet, I
promised myself that if I could make it all the way back
home, this time I would not be leaving again. I renew this
promise now while walking up the road, moving away from
McAllister's store and the silent chorus on the porch, past
the three or four houses that sit ponderously on either side
of the road north of the bus stop and south of the white
Congregational church and the dirt road just beyond the
church on the left, the road that leads to the northern,
narrow end of the valley. I am limping. I am limping, but
while my disabled leg slows me somewhat, it doesn't tire me,
and I think nothing of walking the three and one half miles
from McAllister's in the village to my father's house at the
north end of the valley. With Ché in Guatemala I have walked
from the Izabel Lake to San Agustin Acasaquastlán, crossing
the highest peaks in Guatemala, walking, machete in hand,
through clotted jungle for twenty days without stopping,
walking from sunrise till sunset every day, eating only in the
morning before leaving camp and at night just before falling

into exhausted sleep. We never, in three years, set up a fixed camp, and that is why the Guatemalan Army, with their CIA and American army advisors, never caught up with us. We kept on the move constantly, like tiny fish in an enormous, green sea. . . .

I know that receding behind me, shrinking smaller and smaller in the distance, there are four old men who are trying to figure out who I am, where I've come from, and why I have come from there to Crawford. They hope to stumble onto the first—who I am—and from that to infer the other two. As soon as one of them, probably Dr. Cotton (he would be the youngest of the four, the one with the most reliable memory), figures out who I am, and then that I have come home to Crawford again, maybe this time for good, as soon as they have discovered that much of my identity, they will try to discover the rest—where I have been and what I have been doing all these years.

"How long's it been since he last took off, Doc? Five, six years?"

"No, no, it's five years, actually. As I recall now, it was back in sixty-seven he took off for parts unknown. Right after he come up from Florida to see his dad, as I recall it, who was all laid up with a heart attack, y'know. Angina pectoris, if my memory serves me correctly, was what it was. You remember when ol' Sam took sick, don't you? Paralyzed him almost completely. And the boy, he drove all the way up from Florida soon's he heard his dad was in trouble, even quit his fancy job with this big advertising company down there and everything. Just to make sure his dad was okay. Now that's a son for you. A damn sight better than most of the sons these days, let me tell you. Seems the boy stayed around for a few weeks till his dad got back on his feet, y'know, and then he took off again. Nobody around here knew where he went to, though. Just dropped out of sight. . . ."

"How 'bout Boston, Doc? Used to live down in Boston, I heard. You think he went to Boston?"

"Naw, John, we'd a known it if he'd a been in Boston all these years. Word gets out, y'know."

"Wal, Doc, who knows? Maybe this time the boy's come

home for good. He sure looks like he's been through hell,
though, don't he?"

"Smashed his patella, I'd say, Bob, though I couldn't
offer as to how, or how he picked up that scar on his face.
It sure does change his looks, though. I'd a hardly recognized
him if it wasn't for the fact that I was the one who brought
him into the world in the first place."

"I'll tell you, Doc, I'm hoping this time the boy's come
home for good, 'cause the family'll be needin' him up there."

"They sure as hell do, Bob. And by gawd, we need him
down here, too. . . ."

No. Erase that remark. Wipe it out. Doc would never think
such a thing, let alone say it, and Bob McAllister hates and
distrusts me, I'm sure. Won't even give me credit for a dollar's
worth of gasoline. Be damned if I want to help those people
out of their misery. If Doc Cotton ever saw me getting off a
bus in Crawford, limping, scarred, back in town again after
a mysterious three-year absence (five?), he'd fear for my
family's peace of mind, and, panic-stricken, he'd be on the
phone, as soon as I was safely out of sight, warning them to
be careful. . . .

But that's okay, that's okay now, because everything is
different. I'm about thirty-five, say. Maybe thirty-six, but
no older. I'm about thirty-five, say, and I'm wearing khaki
trousers, a white shirt, open at the throat, and high brown
workshoes that have steel toes. My hair is cut fairly short,
and my face and the backs of my hands are deeply tanned. I
look like a construction worker, except for the limp and the
scar, and when you are a tall, cold-looking man who looks
like a construction worker, except that you limp badly and
bear a cruel machete-scar across your face, what do people
think? They think they're looking at a veteran of guerrilla
warfare, that's what they think. . . .

Okay. So here's these four old turtles sitting in the sun
on McAllister's porch, and the Boston-to-Montreal bus
wheezes up, stopping ostensibly to let off the Boston papers
as usual, but instead of just the wire-bound packet of Boston
Globes, Herald-Travelers, and *Record-Americans* being pitched
out the door, I get off too, first chucking my duffle bag down

the steps ahead of me. The bus driver, moving quickly to give
me a hand, is sent back to his seat by my giving him a fierce,
prideful glare, which silently says to him: *I can make it on
my own.* "Okay . . . ," he says, almost calling me Soldier, but
suddenly thinking better of it, sensing somehow that I have
fought not for a nation, but for a *people*, and thus have worn
no uniform, have worn only what the people themselves, the
peasants, wear. . . .

I like the idea of not having a car, of arriving by bus,
carrying everything I own in a single duffle bag and owning
nothing that can't be left out in the rain. No household goods
are carried on *my* back, no sir. Just a duffle, U.S. Army surplus, brought all the way home from the jungles of Guatemala. And inside it—two changes of clothing, a copy (in a
waterproof plastic bag) of Régis Debray's *Révolution dans
la Révolution*, which has been as a bible to me. Also in a
waterproof plastic bag, the notes for my book (Did I come
back to Crawford for this, to write my own book, a book about
my experiences with Ché in Guatemala, a book which in actu-
ality would be a theoretical textbook thinly disguised as a
memoir and which eventually, it is hoped, would replace the
writings of Debray, Geuvara, Chairman Mao, and even Lenin?).
And the ten essentials: maps (of Belknap County, New Hampshire, obtainable from the National Geological Survey, Washington, D.C.), a good compass, a flashlight, sunglasses, emergency
rations (raisins, chick-peas, and powdered eggs), waterproofed
matches, a candle for fire-starting, a U.S. Army surplus
blanket, a pocketknife, and a small first-aid kit, That's it.
Everything I own in the world is there. The ten essentials. No, I
need to have another: I need one of those small one-man Boy
Scout cooking kits. And maybe I should have a gun, a small
handgun. A black, snub-nosed .38, maybe. I would've had
trouble, though, with the customs officials in Mexico City—
especially since they would've been alerted that I might be coming through and would be carrying something important and
dangerous, like secret instructions from Ché to supporters and
sympathizers inside the U.S. Maybe I should leave Mexico from
Mérida, crossing overland from Guatemala through the low
jungles of the Yucatan in hundred degree heat, walking all
the way, and then suddenly appearing in the line of Ameri-

can tourists checking out of Mérida for Miami. It's when you arrive inside the United States that they check your baggage. They never bother you when you leave a place, only when you come back.

Say I picked up the gun *after* I arrived in Miami, picked it up in a pawn shop. Say I managed to lose the agent assigned to follow me, ducked into an obscure little pawn shop in the west end of the city, and purchased a .38 revolver for twenty-seven fifty. Later, at the airport coffee shop, I spot the agent. He's seated three tables from me, pretending to read his paper while waiting, like me, for his plane to New York. He pretends to read, and he watches my every move. I get up from my chair, leave a small tip, walk over to him and say quietly: "I'm leaving now." Then smile and leave. Probably they would arrest me at some point during my journey, but they would be unable to muster proof that I have been working in Guatemala with Ché for these three— no, five—years. They lost me in Mexico City back in '67, and so far as they can say for sure, that is, so far as they can legally prove, I've been in Mexico all that time. At least twice or three times a year, I slip back across the border to make my presence in Mexico known to the officials—I simply let myself be seen conspicuously drunk in a well-known restaurant—and then, taking off at night from a field near Cuernavaca in a small Beechcraft Bonanza piloted by a mercenary, a gun-runner from New Orleans, I return to the jungles of Guatemala. I am valuable to Ché for many reasons, one of which is my American citizenship, and so it is very important that I do not become *persona non grata*, at least not officially. "Conejo," Ché calls me, using my code name. "Conejo, you are valuable man to me y también a la revolución como soldad, pero también como norteaméricano usted es muy importante, y esa noche hay que volver a México y estar borracho en los restaurantes. ¿Comprendes, amigo?"

"Sí, Ché, yo comprendo." We embrace each other man-fully, the way Latins will, and I leave with the pilot, slashing through the jungle to his plane, which he has cleverly camou-flaged at the edge of a small clearing several miles down the valley from where we have camped. . . .

Now, three thousand miles away. I have just disembarked, from a Greyhound bus in Crawford, New Hampshire. I stand next to the idling bus for a few moments, gazing passively at the scene before me, and upon receiving simultaneously the blows of so much that is familiar and so much that subtly has grown strange to me, I become immobilized. Seeing them, I remember things that I didn't know I had forgotten, and thus I experience everything that comes into my sight as if somehow it were characterized both as brand new, virginally so, and yet also as clearly, reassuringly, familiar. It would be the way my own face, my very own face, appeared to me when, after having grown a beard and worn it for almost two years, I went into a barber shop and asked to have it shaved off. And because I had to lie back in the chair and look up at the ceiling while the barber first snipped with scissors and then shaved with a razor, I was unable to watch my beard gradually disappearing, with my face concurrently appearing from behind it, and when I was swung back down into a seated position and was allowed to peer at my face for the first time in several years, I was stunned by the familiarity of my own face, and also by the remarkable strangeness of it.

THE INVESTITURE

I am down on my knees, holding the body, like the
Virgin in the Pietá holding the dead Christ. I have draped
the corpse across my lap. Something about his face is shock-
ingly familiar, unpleasantly so, but this is probably because
of its vague resemblance to my own—the same broad but
angle-filled face, a face like a cut crystal, with the same tiny
ears and short nose, the full, down-slashed mouth, with the
drooping, Irish eyes, the tangled mop of sandy-grey hair—
except that I am wearing a full beard, and he, as always, is
without one. Also, he is well-dressed, and, of course, I am
not. He wears an expensive, Italian-made, wool suit, light-
weight, with fine black pinstripes over impeccable navy blue;
his suit is rumpled, however, unbuttoned and slightly stained
with a white, mucous-like substance on the breast and side
pockets, as if someone with street filth on his hands has gone
through the pockets hurridly.
      Anticipating a cramp that's about to seize my right thigh
and calf muscles, I shift his weight, with my arms sliding the
body a bit to the left—rocking back on my heels as I slide
the corpse—until I have balanced the weight of it gingerly
atop my knees. He's heavy, but not that heavy, certainly not
what I'd expected. It's almost as if we were underwater,
except that he does not look like a drowned man. More like
a man hit mere seconds ago by a small truck, bumped by the
fender closest to the sidewalk, sending him careening backwards through the dense, noon air, and down, with the tender
back of his head striking the edge of the curb, one blow, a
dull thud switching at once into a click, and he is dead, the
only mark on his body a finger-sized, blue indentation just
above the medulla oblongata, and that thatched over by his
much-adored, tousled, sandy-grey hair.

He's not wearing a necktie, doubtless because of walking these streets at midday. The Long Hot Summer, they'd called it, with resigned anticipation. It was going to be A Long Hot Summer. Conflagrations, riots, shootings, lootings, rapes—Oh, they'd expected the worst to happen, all of them. And when he started taking these midday walks, talking and shaking hands, touching bodies with the natives as he strolled along the crowded streets, moving swiftly through the bazaars and temporary encampments, as if by magic closing all the rips and tears that run erratically through the body of any people,—when he began, the ones at the palace had at first laughed loudly.

But their laughter swiftly turned to warnings and dark prophecy. "No, no, Sweet Prince," they implored him, "stay here with *us*, behind the walls! Don't go out there, unarmed and unguarded, they'll slay you, they'll rend your beautiful body, and as the crescendo to some riotous, barbaric rite, they'll devour the dripping pieces! No, stay here, and listen with us to the sweet lutes in the afternoons and the smooth, cool click of the chess pieces as they slide across the ivory boards. Stay and speak wittily with us of the changes in our currency and the subtle evolution of forms. We need your sober, informed, anciently entitled force among us. We need to regard your extraordinary face and admire the way you wear fine clothes. Stay with us, gather the beautiful laughing young women around you, and drive with us in white convertibles between the inner and outer walls where the sunlight falls all day long!"

But he waved them off, shook them off his back like a young stallion shaking off an unskilled rider, and walked out the huge, center gate and disappeared into the maze of tiny, involuted streets and rickety shops, submerged by the babbling knots of citizens, exotically garbed tent-dwellers hawking their wares, devious moneylenders and mercenaries striking illicit bargains, young men and short-haired women plotting minor outrage and debauch, families settling ancient, tribal quarrels in the public squares. All of these were at first shocked into momentary silence by the sight of the tall, fair, elegantly proportioned and gently smiling Leader, the Sweet Prince, a silence that was immediately followed by renewed noise, an even greater buzz and babble of human voice than

before. "It *was* he, indeed! I saw him myself, and he had gone
past me before I realized that I was seeing him, in the flesh
and not just some clever poster pasted to a stucco wall! He
was among us! Walking, alone and unarmed, *here*, among *us*!
I do not lie! I would know that face, that fine figure, that
shock of tousled, sandy-grey hair—I have seen his *picture*
often enough!

"And to think that I had almost begun to believe that
story, the one about his having been killed by a highly placed
minister, years ago, a man who had none of the divine peroga-
tive and knew it, so he kept the image of the Sweet Prince
always before us, issued edicts and proclamations in his name,
even posed a look-alike for public appearances (the few times
in the last decade that he had been seen publicly, it was
always from a great distance—inside a curtained coach or at
a balcony high up in the outer wall). But now, after seeing
him walking so calmly and . . . happily, so gently concerned,
walking here among us . . . well, now I know that he is still
our Leader and that he truly loves us! He shook the hand of
my eldest son, he offered an affectionate, slightly lustful
look to my wife, and he gave me his respect. And then he
was gone, swallowed by the crowd and the narrow, crooked
streets jammed with the people and their animals and their
vehicles and their refuse. . . ."

A priest has come to stand before me. With one hand, he
holds a large, plain, gold cross diagonally across his breast,
and with the other hand an ornate, gold scepter. He wears the
high, heaven-pointing hat of a cardinal, the long, scarlet and
ermine robes, with exquisitely crafted lace fringing his cuffs
and the bottom edges of his robes, clustering like an orchid
at his blotched, spongy throat.

With nets of tiny, purple veins sprawling across his cheeks
and nose, langorous earlobes dangling against his neck, he
smiles condescendingly down at my upturned face. He is
mocking my tears. I lift the body a few inches off my lap,
as if to explain my weeping, but he acknowledges nothing.
At a vague distance, there is a large crowd of anonymous,
peasant faces ringing us. Clearly, they are in the Cardinal's
power, and if he decides to say aloud that *I* am the one who
slew the Sweet Prince, they will rush upon me and will tear

my living body into a hundred pieces, and they will jam the
still-bleeding chunks of flesh into their mouths and ears and
grind them against their groins and breasts, urinating, defe-
cating, masturbating onto the last bits and pieces of my body.

"Father, I am not Catholic," I inform him meekly.

"No. You're not." His voice is whiskeyed, gravelly, flat as
a sun-baked stone. "But that won't immunize you." He smiles,
caps a tiny belch with yellowed teeth. "No. You're a Protestant. That's a far cry from some foreign diplomat merely
caught in a mildly embarrassing situation, eh?" He smiles
slightly for a second, admiring the intricacies of the trap.

"I followed him down here. He didn't know."

"Oh?" Smiling again, twitching his nose, the talcum
powder on his shaved cheeks and chin streaked with sweat.
He steals a quick look over his shoulder at the crowd, as if
checking its now restive mood against his earlier impression.

"I . . . I was the only one who saw him die, Father. No
one else, for that brief moment, was in the street. It was
suddenly deserted, this short street before you now. He
recognized me. He must have realized that I had been following him, and for an instant he ignored the hazards of walking
in the middle of a city street at midday. And that's when this
little Japanese truck came barreling around the corner. The
corner right over there, Father, next to the leather goods
shop. The truck struck him a glancing blow with its near
fender, sending him flying backwards against the curb. By
the time I got to him, the truck was gone. Gone. And he
was dead. It all happened so quickly, Father. . . . "

"And the driver?" he asks, his voice thin with disbelief.
"Did you happen to see the driver?"

"Only for an instant, a flash. The truck swung past me
and sped around that far corner there, and disappeared. But
I saw the driver as the truck passed me. A tall man, he
seemed, gaunt, broad-faced, but craggy-featured, you know?
Kind of lantern-jawed, with a prominent forehead and cheek-
bones, deep-set eyes, blue eyes they were. And a short,
Roman nose, very small ears, a mop of unkempt, light brown,
greying hair. And a thick moustache, Father. No scars or
other identifying marks. No moles. But I'd know him if I ever
saw him again. You can believe that!"

"All right. Thank you, we'll notify you if we decide to need you." Very brusquely now, the Cardinal turns and orders four of the larger men in the crowd to come over and take the corpse away from me and carry it up to the palace. They do as they are instructed, and the Cardinal turns and leaves, leading the procession—the Cardinal, then the bearers of the body of the Sweet Prince, holding it at shoulder height, four burly men walking in lock-step, as if trained precisely for this instant, and then the crowd, a huge, blossoming mass of dark, somber men, women and children, silent in their awe-struck grief.

With the possible exception of the Cardinal, no one who was in the city that afternoon had ever been so close to an actual historical event and known it at the time. We all wanted it to last forever. When they were gone from sight, I began quietly to moan, and oh, I moaned until dark, when I must have fallen asleep, for when I woke, it was almost dawn, and the shop-keepers were beginning to unlock their doors and set out their wares again. I picked myself up from the filth of the gutter and walked straight home to the palace, washed, shaved, dressed gorgeously in black and made a somber, perfunctory appear-ance at breakfast. No one seemed to suspect a thing. The funeral, the brief period of mourning afterwards, the inaugura-tion, the reconvening of the legislature and the courts—all went smoothly, like clockwork. There was an investigation, of course. (After all, certain proprieties must be honored.) But everyone seemed content with the investigating panel's con-clusion that the Sweet Prince, our late, much-lamented leader, had been slain accidentally by a man driving a foreign-made automobile, a "pathetic loner", an "unknown psychopath", who, as soon as he realized whom he had slain, had fled the country and disappeared completely. As for me, I never go outside the outer walls anymore. Once in a lifetime is enough. When you become Leader, you're suddenly the only person left who is still interested in imagining the pain of your own death. For everyone else, it's history.

THE BLIZZARD

A low, mottled grey sky, smooth and unbroken in texture. The man stands, hands in pockets, next to the neatly stacked, headhigh woodpile, looking first up at the sky, then down to his feet, and he smiles beneath his thick moustache and shakes his head, as if remembering something that had been funny long ago and only to him. Taking long strides, he crosses behind the barn and walks along the side opposite the house, moving gracefully through high, brown meadow-grass to the front, where the driveway ends. As he passes near the car, a Volkswagen sedan, he flips his hand down and without breaking his stride raps the vehicle once on the roof. He is tall, not heavy, with a large head made even larger by the bushy, dark brown moustache that droops across his lower face. He moves with a strange, hurried grace: there is an urgency to his walk and in the slightly forward tilt of his shoulders and head, as if he has not been able to make himself altogether comfortable inside his body. His large, heavy hands swing with relaxed precision, however. He can reach out great distances and touch quickly, without first having to think of it, whatever he wants to touch. They are the kind of hands that would be good with tools but clumsy with the buttons of his own clothing. He walks to the side entrance of the house, reaches forward and opens the door before his foot has arrived at the step outside the door, and as he brings the rest of his body into the house, he grins and says into the kitchen, We'll have snow tomorrow. Then he closes the door behind him.

When I become cold, it begins in my feet and fingertips and quickly moves in from there. As long as those far extremities

are warm, even if I have no hat or coat on, the rest of my
body stays comfortably warm. Before I grew my moustache,
my face was the first part of my body to feel the cold.

He reached down and across the kitchen table and grabbed
his wife's arm just above the elbow and yanked her to her
feet, shaking her once, holding her elbow high in the air so
that she seemed to dangle from it. The flesh of her face
stiffened and drew forward protectively like a hood, her
head pulled down close to her shoulders, her one free hand
clutching vainly at the hard, outside surface of his viselike
grip, and when he bellowed into her face, she began to sob.
I'm sorry, I'm sorry, I don't know what else to do! she cried.
Then he bellowed a second time. Just be quiet! You are
making us miserable over nothing! *Nothing*!

This seems to be how the winter works on me, and what
follows immediately from that work. First, I lose my hold
on my sense of my self, then of my life as some kind of continuing history. Then of my wife, and finally, of my children.
The progression goes on out from there, until at last, by the
time the first trickles of spring appear, I am like a vaguely
discolored fluid floating on the surface of a stagnant sea.
      The how and the what, then, are always easy to say and
understand. The difficult question, the true question here,
is *why*.
      It's difficult for me even to ask it, not to mention
answering, for every time and as soon as I do ask it, I know
that I'm no longer talking about the weather. If the answer
in fact did have anything to do with the weather, if it somehow were able to explain to me the agressive workings of the
winter upon my mind's hold on itself and the world, if it
were able to show me that from November to April I was
being ravished by nothing more than the incessant waves of
snow and cold—then it would be a simple matter to move
to another climate. I would merely move my chair closer to
the fire.
      But I don't do that. I keep my chair where it has always
been. On the north side of the house and as close to the door
as possible. Which confuses me, confuses me now, today,

when winter has just begun. In a month, of course, I won't be confused, at least not in this particular way, because the question will have been lost and I will have given up the search for it. In two months I will have forgotten that there ever existed such a question. I'll be unable to speak of it.

The problem, for me and in many ways for the people around me, is that when I *am* able to speak of it, that is, in the fall and at the beginning of winter, it's only because I've just regained my full strength. I believe this. The spring and summer healings have brought me to a point by late fall where once again I feel like a solid block of ice, and the world around me has distinction and, of itself, variety. This for me is a time of unabated pleasure, which can be broken only by my reminding myself of how precarious a time it is, and how brief.

What's going on? my wife has asked me. No, really, what the hell is going on?

I don't know what you mean. Nothing. (There's little else I can say at such times.)

You know damned well what I mean. This *silent* bit. It's not exactly something new to me, you know. It could be kind of cute, if I happened to be meeting you for the first time. But I'm not meeting you for the first time. I'm your wife, remember? And we've been together like this for quite a while now. So what's going on?

Nothing. (I was sitting in the chair by the kitchen door, waterproofing my boots with Neatsfoot Oil. At daybreak the snow had started falling. Now, three hours later, two inches of hard, fine powder had accumulated.)

Who are you? Gary Cooper? Can't you say anything more than *nothing*? I've heard nothing but monosyllabics out of you for the past three weeks!

Sorry. (I pulled my boots over my Norwegian wool socks.)

My wife sat down at the far end of the kitchen table, her elbows on the table and her chin resting on her fisted hands. She looked slightly angry, flirting with fear. Are you going to *talk* to me? I know something's happened, I've been through this before with you. We both have.

What are you talking about? I asked, standing in my

boots, wiggling my toes inside. (When your feet are comfortable, your entire body relaxes and enjoys your feet's
small pleasure vicariously.)

You *know* what I'm talking about! *Guilt!* She hissed the
word at me without moving her lips or teeth, and I knew
that she had flopped over, from anger to fear.

Ridiculous, I said, smiling.

Don't you take me lightly.

I'm not. You're simply wrong. That's all. There's nothing
the matter, and there's nothing going on. I just haven't had
much to say lately, that's all. Been busy and kind of pre-
occupied, I guess.

Really? she said, sneering. Well, I *know* you, mister, and
I know what it means when you go silent on me. If you're
wise, you'll talk to me, and you'll do it now, while I can still
be sympathetic. We've been through all this before, too many
times, and we both know what the consequences are, and we
both know how to avoid those consequences. So *talk!*

Listen, I said. I've got to spend all day cutting wood for
the stoves and shoveling snow. We can't spend all day talking
about something that doesn't exist. Tonight we'll talk, if you
still think there's something going on. But really, it's nothing.

Yes, I'm sure that's what you think. And that's why
you're keeping silent, so you can go on thinking that it's
nothing. For once in our lives, I ought to let you go ahead
and try living with your silent self. If I had enough distance
on you, believe me, I'd just keep quiet and let your silence
take you as far as it could. Then, finally, you might believe
me when I tell you something's happened.

Wal, I can't say as how I believe you this morning. And
since we happen to be discussing *my* life, I guess I'll just have
to act as the final authority. I gave her a friendly smile.

She grimly said nothing. I put on my coat and went out
into the snow. Usually, when I go from the house to the barn,
I go by way of the connecting shed—the long, narrow structure that runs like an umbilical cord from the house to the
barn, a building that yearly comes a little bit closer to approx-
imating a finished studio,—but this time, with the first snow
falling, I wanted to come into my studio from outside, stamping my feet and brushing snow off my sleeves, shedding the
heavy coat and going right to work.

The man stumbles into the carpeted lobby of the motel, waking the half-asleep room clerk with the blast of wind and snow that enters with him. The clerk looks up at the man, who towers above the impeccable counter—a tall man, hatless, wearing a dark blue wool overcoat, ice and snow laid down in thick strips across his head and shoulders. He plops his scarlet hands heavily on the counter in front of the clerk, a small, old man wearing a flannel shirt and wool necktie. Forty-seven, the man in the overcoat says. His voice is low and soft, and he speaks slowly. I'm in room forty-seven. He goes into his pocket, and drawing out his room key, dangles it in front of the clerk's wide-open face. I want two things, the man says. Yes, sir, the clerk answers. First, my car. It's stuck downtown on Main Street, right next to a place called The Home Port. It's a black Volkswagen sedan and can be towed back here easily. Do you know of someone you can get at this hour who'll tow my car back here? The clerk nods. Good. The second thing I want is to be wakened at six. The clerk zips out his ball point pen and writes down carefully, *Wake 47 at 6:00.* Is that it? he asks. Yes, the man answers. He reaches into his pocket again, this time pulling out his wallet, and hands the clerk a five dollar bill. This is to cover your trouble in making sure my car gets back here tonight. I assume the towing charges can be added to my bill. Right, the old man says. We have a kid with a jeep here all night, plowing, you know. He'll run down and get your car for you. All right, the man says. I'll be checking out in the morning. Yes, sir, the clerk answers. Good night, sir.

Listen to me, it's fine for you to lie there and tell me all about my kind of guilt syndrome, you can tell me about it all night long, and I'll lie quietly next to you and listen closely and with gratitude. You're an extremely intelligent woman who's blessed with remarkable insight. I can appreciate all that. God knows how important to both of us your particular insights into my guilt syndrome have been. Frankly, they've managed to save our marriage. I can confess that. No, really, I *must* confess that. I don't want to end up feeling guilty for unspoken gratitude, do I? No. Okay, then. What I was saying is that it's all well and good for you to lie there and tell me how convoluted my guilt syndrome is, how

I bury it with wordy evasions, lies, rationalizations and buck-
passing, and it's all right for you to observe to me that one of
my most effective devices, when confronted by something
for which I must feel guilty, is simple silence and outright
detachment. You're right about all that. I'm not arguing
with you over that. I concede it. Personally, I think that
these are the kinds of insights on your part that have saved
our marriage. I don't think we'd be married today if you
hadn't pushed them into my face, again and again. I mean
this. Ten years we've been married, and if it hadn't been for
your persistance and your patience in making the truth of
these insights evident to me, we wouldn't have been married
for more than the first three years. A lot of growth. Lots of
changes. On both our parts. And mine have had to come in
just this area, over my inability to handle guilt. But to get
back to what I was saying, just because my usual response to
a guilt-situation *is* silence and detachment, this does not
mean conversely that, whenever I've gone silent on you and
seem to be detached and withdrawn, I am reacting to conscious knowledge of some offense I've committed. No. It's
quite possible, see, that I can turn silent and can *seem* withdrawn for no reason that has anything to do with any offense
or guilt. Okay, so then you'll come back at me and argue,
with justification, I admit, that for me guilt is general and
not particular, that I don't need a specific offense in order
to feel challenged by guilt, that it's part of my entire consciousness of my relation to the rest of the world. This may
be true, it *is* true, I suspect. But what we're talking about
here are *symptoms. Effects.* Not causes. You can argue from
causes out to effects if you want to, but when it comes to
my guilt syndrome, you've got no right to start arguing backwards from the effects. After all, my silence and my seeming
detachment can be caused by many things. What if I had a
stroke or something and couldn't speak at all? What would
you say then, that I was avoiding coming to grips with my
guilt-consciousness? Did you ever think of that, missus? Or
what if I were grieving? What if, just as an example, I
happened to be holding some terrible news about *your*
health? That you had terminal cancer, say? Maybe I'm
worried about my work, maybe I'm not going to be able

to make the mortgage payment. You haven't asked me, you know. All you've done is assume that I'm acting out of some convoluted guilt syndrome again. I've been unusually silent these past few weeks, you tell me, and I seem to be uninvolved with you, with your daily life. Okay. Fine. So I'm a little less communicative than usual. There might be lots of reasons for that. You might try asking me what *I* think, you know. And so I *seem* to be uninvolved with your daily life. That's *your* impression. Which, as far as I can see, could as easily be a simple insecurity on your part as something concretely true of my behavior. In other words, my seeming detachment could as much be a false impression as a true one, depending on whether or not it's a direct result of your fearful assumption that my silence, which *is* concretely true of my behavior, is a symptom of my difficulties in dealing with a rather extreme sense of personal guilt. So what, if I happen to have difficulties in dealing with a rather extreme sense of personal guilt? That's *my* problem, isn't it? Not yours. Silence and detachment aren't exactly the worst things a woman has to bear in most marriages, you know. I mean, it's only a *temporary* silence, and it's never more than a failed attempt at detachment. You know this. Eventually, I always start to talk again, little by little, evasively, I know, but eventually I circle back to you, and from there to my particular offense and guilt, and from there to my general guilt. You've never seen it work any other way, have you? I might ask what the hell you're afraid of in the first place. In this case here, you can be sure that if there *were* some particular offense I had committed, I would finally return to it, would confess it to you, would admit that, yes, I did make a pass at Rose, as she claimed I did, for example. Just for example. And once there, you can rest assured that I would admit that I had overreacted, had treated a particular, small offense as if it were a general, lifelong one, that therefore I had reacted to a minor offense in terms of my consciousness of an overall guilt. I mean, this is what has always happened, isn't it? No exceptions. None whatsoever, not in ten years. So why are you so determined now to conclude from my silence and my *seeming* detachment that I necessarily must be reacting to a failure to confront my guilt for a

minor offense? You don't have to worry about it, because if
I were, you'd know it by now. You always have. Why is this
any different? What are you afraid of? That something dread-
ful will happen if you don't push and shove me back over the
past few weeks all the way to some forgotten, ignored, completely minor offense against you? What the hell are you
afraid of?

She told me to shut my god-damned mouth. Shut your god-
damned mouth. Low and level, the words came out like looping circles of rope that cleanly hooped one after the other
around my head, and I shut my god-damned mouth. The
others in the room, also women, stared quickly down at the
coffee cup cluttered tabletop between them, fingered their
paper napkins. One of them, Rose, I think, said, Jesus, it's
hot by this stove, and moved her chair without getting out
of it, bumping it against the floor of the kitchen, down the
side of the rectangular table and away from the woodstove.
My wife got up and with a sharp twist turned the damper
down and returned to her chair without looking at me. They
went back to what they had been talking about—Rose's
mother. The three women, my wife, tall and dark, and her
two shorter, unmarried friends, leaning intently across the
kitchen table, fooling with coffee cups and paper napkins
and cigarettes, one or two of the three talking in pleasant,
intimate voices about a mother: as if I had not just come in
from the barn demanding to know who in hell had left the
water running, because the goddamned pump was sucking
air again, and for Christ's sake, the water was not supplied
by a public utility and if the well goes dry we'll be up shit's
creek, and it meant that now I'd have to shut off the pump
and leave us without any water at all for hours, until the
pipe fills back up, *if* the pipe fills back up, and *if* the god-
damned pump hasn't already burned itself out from sucking
air for God knows how long. What the hell's the matter with
you? I asked her. Can't you hear the grinding noise it makes
when it starts to suck air? And it was also as if at that
moment my wife had not told me to shut my god-damned
mouth.
     Where are you going? was what she said, almost casually,

as I stomped across the kitchen and pulled my coat off the hook by the door. I glared at her. Then I stuffed my arms into the heavy coat, yanked open the door and stalked into the blowing snow, closing the door with a quick jerk, as if pulling my hand out of a pan of hot water.

The Volkswagen started gradually, reluctantly, stiff in the late afternoon cold, but it started. While the motor warmed up, I got out of the car and thrashed through the piling snow and with my bare hand brushed the windows clean. Coming around from the far side of the car, I caught a glimpse of my wife's face at the kitchen door. She was staring quizzically through the small square window in the door, as if at the weather. Then she turned away and disappeared. I got into the car, backed it slowly down the driveway to the road, leaving foot-deep ruts in the snow behind me, then drove lurchingly away, plowing carelessly through the small, shifting drifts. A half-mile of unpaved, snow-banked road, the car busting the fast-building drifts that lined the inside edge of the snowbanks, spraying high, white foxtails over the fenders, and I was on the main road. It was nearly dark, so I switched on the headlights. Turning left, I headed toward Portsmouth. The main road had already been plowed (huge orange plows would cruise up and down the road from Portsmouth to Concord all night long), and consequently the driving was much easier than I had anticipated.

Although I am in love with the woman, the pressure of living with her doesn't let up, even after ten years. The kind of pressure I'm talking about has nothing to do with being *me*, or being male even, yet it can't be the same for her, because of the fact that she is *there*, on the one hand, and is talking, constantly talking, prodding, shoving, probing, on the other. The words alone would not be sufficient to box me in. The words alone, when they happen to be true (that is, accurate), merely disappear as quickly as they're uttered; and when they're not true, the words, *her* words, just fall to our feet and flop over on their sides, dead, like so many flat slab-sided carp. But the fact that she is *there*, separate from me, yet distinctly *there*, undeniably so, coupled with the fact that she is talking, talking, talking—these two constantly present

tense facts produce in me the need to answer, and suddenly
I find myself boxing myself in with my *own* words. They
swirl out of my mouth like an odor, and as soon as they have
separated themselves from my body, they solidify, as if by
magic, and make a wall. Then more words follow, making a
wall inside the first. Then still more words, and yet another,
nearer wall. Until my body has been jammed into a rectangular
cube of precisely my body's volume. No more, no less. And
comfortless, I go silent.

And as a result, over the years the women who have
attracted me more and more frequently have been silent
women. I think . . . no, I'm *sure* that I was attracted to Rose,
for example, purely and simply because of her silence. She
almost never speaks, except to refer to some particular,
physical circumstance. I am cold. I am too warm. I am tired.
I am not tired. And so on. In place of words, Rose offers
an infinite number of tones of silence, each of which, when
observed, can be understood in countless ways. She smiles
with her lips, and I start asking myself, *Wanly? Condescend-*
ingly? Coyly? Idly? Cruelly? Seductively? In other words,
she creates for me the possibilities of a specific attitude
towards me, an attitude she will gladly bear, yet one that
I am free to determine. *Seductively*, I decide, with a bit of
Coyly tempered with *Idly*. And so I go ahead and place my
two hands onto her waist, sliding them down to her hips,
pulling her to me, and as she turns her face up to mine, her
eyes wide open, I kiss her on the mouth and ear and throat.

That was all. I didn't make love to her (my wife was in
the kitchen, getting ice from the refrigerator, Rose and I
were standing in the middle of the livingroom, Rose's boyfriend, the grade school teacher, was in the bathroom, flush-
ing the toilet while pissing, to cover the splash of his urine's
fall into the water). I let go of Rose, went over to the record
player and put on a record; she went back to reading the
titles on the spines of the books. Now that it's about to
begin, I said to her from my corner of the room (just as my
wife came in with the ice), what do you think of our New
Hampshire winters? Not much, she said, smiling at the books.
They begin too early, and from what I've heard, they last
too long, she said.

We talked that way, in code, for the entire evening, right in front of my wife and Rose's grade school teacher boyfriend. My wife, more beautiful than Rose, grew bored rather early and, as a result, silent, and by ten she was yawning and making sleepy references to how early she had to get up to get the kids ready in time for school. Rose's boyfriend (whose name I could not remember for longer than thirty seconds at a time) spent the evening in unrelenting, embarrassed discomfort, mainly, I think, because of my (to him) haggard appearance. And, too, I did make a number of unnecessary references both to waterfalls and to the noisy plumbing of the house, how you could hear water gushing, like a waterfall, all through the house every time someone flushed the toilet. I remember that he wanted badly to tell me all about his mother's having recently taken up ceramics, at the remarkable age of sixty-four. But I kept interrupting him with the story of my friend's arthritic thumb and forefinger on his left hand, the way he had turned their dead rigidity to his advantage as a potter, adding several times that arthritis can actually aid a potter in his work, as long as it affects no more than a couple of fingers and doesn't stiffen an entire hand. He pretended to be relieved to hear that. I smiled. He and Rose left early. My wife and I made love for a long time and fell asleep immediately after and together.

After phoning my wife from the motel, informing her that I had no intentions of coming home again as long as she remained there, I went out to look for a woman. My plan had been simply to drive to downtown Portsmouth, and avoiding the bars that catered strictly to seamen, to find a crowded neighborhood bar. I pictured a woman slightly older than I, in her late thirties, say, or maybe around forty, still attractive, and lonely, because her husband would be at sea, either on a fishing boat off the Grand Banks or else assigned as chief petty officer to a Navy training ship based in Portsmouth and on winter maneuvers somewhere east of Norfolk. That was my plan. I would talk to her with sympathy and intelligence, buying her drinks, and when the bar closed at one A. M., we'd stroll down the street, arm in arm, like the good friends that we would have become by

then, to her small, cozy apartment, where, before we went to
bed, she'd make me a cup of tea. We would talk quietly for
a few minutes longer. Then we'd make love, and it would be
gently exhilerating to both of us, and afterwards we'd fall
into a deep, peaceful sleep. In the morning I would decide
what I was going to do with the wreckage of my life. I
would talk about it with her, and she would give me sound
advice.

    I had not anticipated the blizzard, however. For that's
what it had become, a true blizzard. It was still November,
the winter's first snowfall—usually amounting to little more
than an inch or two of light powder that melts the next day—
but by the time I got to the Holiday Inn outside Portsmouth,
after a harrowing forty mile drive, over a foot of snow had
accumulated, and it was beginning to come down in large,
wet blossoms. I must have ignored these facts and their im-
plications, because when I came out of the motel room and
got into the car again, I was astonished to see that the windshield was completely covered with snow, even though the
motor (and the windshield wipers) had been shut off for
not more than three or four minutes—just long enough for
me to go into the room, close the door behind me, cross to
the telephone table between the beds, and dialing the number
of my home telephone, say to my wife, This is to tell you
that I'm not coming home tonight, so don't wait up for me.

    What? When *are* you coming home, then? Her voice was
small and sounded very far away.

    I can't hear you, I said.

    I said when *are* you coming home, then?

    Well, I guess I won't be coming home as long as you're
there.

    Do you mean that?

    Yes. I do.

    All right. Then she hung up the phone.

If this indeed was the city of Portsmouth, New Hampshire,
its narrow, crooked streets rapidly disappearing in the snow,
the ledges of the rundown Federalist houses puffing white
in the cold swirl of darkness, the pinched-in sidewalks all
but deserted, the numberless barrooms and restaurants closed

up for the night, an unseasonal night no matter how it was regarded, and if that white, turtle-shaped heap of snow next to me and in the middle of the street was in fact my black Volkswagen, stuck in wet, packed snow that came up to the tops of the hubcaps, if all this was true, then I must have been the person who was standing in the street, the tall man with the tiny icicles in his moustache. He was five miles from the room he had rented at the Holiday Inn (he had wanted to avoid the rooming houses in the city). He was hatless and without gloves, though he did have on a pair of insulated, leather boots. He started walking, slowly at first, then at a faster pace, and soon he wasn't cold and was enjoying the night and the snow and the sea-chilled wind that came at him from behind, from the sea, shoving him along his way, helping him, even, so long as he was headed inland. At that time, as he stumbled, walked, and finally jogged happily through the streets of Portsmouth in the middle of a blizzard, I could not believe that I was anyone other than the man with the icicles in his moustache. I was on both sides of his eyes, inside and outside as well, and his eyes were filled with water. It occurred to me that the man might die, that he might have caught pneumonia and was feverish, or that unknowingly he had for years been carrying inside him a killing disease that now, when he was most vulnerable, had decided to strike him down. It occurred to me that he was insane. It occurred to me that he was not insane.

He woke, expecting the storm to be over and the sun to be shining on a soft, white world. It was not over. The sky was still low and mottled grey, the snow blowing from the northeast, the wet air unseasonably, dully cold. The drive back to his house seemed interminable.

THE NAP

Trusting a private tradition, he'd fallen asleep while reading
a recently published novel. His expectation (he'd not realized
he'd held one, until it was not met) had been to waken to a
difference. Any difference. But he'd perceived no difference.
His wife, the nice, very same wife with the wirey hair, was
out in the kitchen, talking angrily to their oldest child, the
girl named Janet. The second child, Roger, was sprawled on
the floor, between him (on his back on the sofa on the rug)
and the cold, black mouth of the fireplace. The boy was
laborously reading the comics section of the Sunday newspaper. It was still Sunday afternoon. His third child, the
daughter Cynthia, was visiting her best friend (he listened to
his wife in the adjacent room as, with irritation, she referred
to that fact). And the dog was still being called outside the
house, because of the smell of the dead skunk. He noted the
fallen planes of light in the dim room, the piles of thick
shadow against the walls, the fireplace, the casual arrange-
ments of furniture, pictures, draperies, and carpets—and he
saw that everything was precisely as he'd left it. He squinted
and checked the book he'd been reading, a popular novel
about a spy for the CIA, a Jew who, stumbling across an ex-
Gestapo officer living incognito in the Bronx, was forced to
confront his own life as a spy by choosing whether to blow
his own cover by turning the ex-Nazi over to the Israelis or
to maintain his identity as an American spy and thereby vio-
late his Jewishness. The book lay open, spine to the ceiling,
on his belly, turned to the page he had been reading when he
had fallen asleep. Staring down at it, from above, as it were,
he began that period of his life when he trusted nothing and
no one and greeted sleep with a wariness that bordered on
hysteria.

WITH CHÉ AT KITTY HAWK

Her first day at Kitty Hawk, she stayed at the cottage with her mother and father and explained to them why she was leaving Roger. They sat on the beach in canvas and aluminum chairs and watched the children play with shovels and buckets at the edge of the water. As if speaking into a tape recorder, the three adults stared straight ahead while they talked to one another. The sun was white, unencumbered, untouched, in a cloudless sky, burning at the center of the dark blue, circular plane.

Bored with buckets and shovels, the two little girls— daughters and granddaughters—put the toys down and moved closer to the water, to dodge the waves, tempting them, dodging again. At first laughing gaily, then slightly frightened by the noise and power of the surf whenever a wave shoved their ankles and knees or as it receded caught them from behind, their laughter suddenly, momentarily, would turn manic, and small, brown faces would shift to grey, mouths gaping, eyes searching the beach for Mamma.

"Jesus, it's like Greece, this sky and that sun!"

"All week," her father said. "It's been like this all week, Janet. Can you believe it?" With leathery, tanned skin, boney face and round, wrinkle-rimmed eyes, he looked like a giant sea turtle ripped cruelly from its shell and thrown into a canvas beach chair. He lay there, rather than sat, staring at his granddaughters, fingertips nervously drumming knobby knees, toes digging into the hot, white sand. "Listen, honey," he finally said, "maybe you can give it one last chance. You've got the children to think about, you know."

"That's all I've *done*, for God's sake, is think about those two children! I mean, figure it out for yourself, Daddy. Are they any better off with one parent who's reasonably sane and

more or less happy, or with two parents, both of whom are
crazy and miserable and blaming their craziness and misery
on each other? Which would *you* have preferred? For that
matter, which do you think *I* would have preferred?" Chewing her upper lip, she still did not look at him, though she
knew the difficulty her questions would cause him, his
inability to answer truthfully, and the weakness that would
not let him force her to restate or withdraw them. She
wondered about herself—Would she become idly cruel?

Her father started to stammer, then inhaled deeply (a
reversed sigh), and talked rapidly about his own mother
and father, reminding himself, his wife and his daughter that
at least once in this life there had been utter success in the
universal attempt to make a perfect marriage. In the middle
of his eulogy, his paean, his wife got up from her chair, wiped
clinging grains of sand from her lumpy calves and hands, and
walked back to the cottage.

"Do you want a drink, Janet?" she called over her sun-
reddened shoulder. The turquoise straps of her bathing suit
were cutting into loaves of flesh.

"God, no, Mother! It's only three o'clock!"

"Yes. What about you, Charles?"

"What? What? Oh! Yeh, fine, fine, Anne. Gin and tonic.
You know."

Silently, the mother turned and waded through the deep
sand, over the low ridge to the cottage. The daughter and
the father continued to sit in the low-slung chairs, side by
side, watching the two little girls playing. For several minutes
the old man and the young woman said nothing.

Then the man sighed loudly, and said, as if to a friendly
bartender, "Jesus, what a goddam shame."

She turned slowly and looked at him. "Yes, it's a goddam
shame. A shame that it took me eight years. That's all *I'm*
ashamed of!" she snapped. She got up from her chair and
jogged down to the water, pounding through the surf until
she was waist-deep, and dove into a breaking wave, disappearing and popping up after several seconds, beyond the wave, in
smooth, dark green, deep water.

She poked one hand up in the air and waved to her father.
He lifted a skinny, brown arm and slowly waved back.

She was what they used to call "a good looker"– neat,
trim, sexy if tanned and wearing carefully selected clothes,
a fashionably casual haircut and minimal makeup (but not
without makeup altogether), the kind of woman whose
attractiveness to men depended greatly on the degree to which
she could reveal that men were attractive to her. If, however,
it turned out that, for whatever reason or length of time,
actually she was not so interested in men, her boyish, physical
intensity repelled them. These were occasions when she was
thought a lesbian, which, on these occasions, pleased her. It
would serve the bastards right, she thought.

Stalking past the bunch of teenaged boys and men in tee
shirts with sleeves rolled up to show off biceps and tattoos
(flat-eyed hunters waiting for the quarry and drinking cans
of beer cooled in styrofoam boxes at their feet), she hurried
to a place about halfway down the Fish Pier. Out at the end
of the pier, the serious fishermen had gathered, fifteen or
twenty of them, redfaced, white men in duck-bill caps and
bright-colored, shortsleeve shirts and bermuda shorts, all of
them leaning like question marks over the waisthigh wood
railing, peering out and down at their lines, silently attentive.

She slipped in between two small groups of black people,
men and women, and stuffing a cold, slumbering bloodworm
onto the hook, leaned over the rail and flipped the tip of the
rod, casting underhanded, sending the weighted hook and
worm forty or fifty feet out and twenty feet down into the
dark water. Slowly, she reeled the line back in, watching the
people around her as she worked.

"How you doin'?" a man with an enormous head asked
her. "Any bites?" He flashed a mouthful of gold-trimmed
teeth.

"No. But I just got here," she said. She heard the words
clicking in a hard, flat, Boston accent. She never heard her
own accent, except when she happened to be speaking with
blacks—no matter, even, that they were blacks from Chicago
or Brooklyn. Southern whites, strangely, only made her conscious of *their* accent, not her own. The same was true for
Puerto Ricans.

The man was with two women, both of whom seemed to
be older than he, and two men, also older than he. None of

the others were fishing. Instead, they drank beer and ate fried
chicken legs and chattered with each other and with the
various black people passing by and standing around them.
The man fishing was, by comparison, a solitary. To support
the impression, he carefully ignored the others, occasionally
chuckling or shaking his head in mock-exasperation. His very
large head was almost startling to look at, all the more (for
a white person) because of his shiney blackness. Janet didn't
realize she was staring at him, at his head, the bludgeon-like
force of it, until, smiling easily at her, he asked, "You know
me, Miss?"

"No, no, I guess not. I just thought, I . . . you do look
familiar to me, that's all."

"You prob'ly seen me around," he said, almost bragging.

"Yes." She noticed that whenever he spoke to her, the
others immediately lapsed into silence—but only for as long
as he was speaking. When she answered him, they went back
to their own conversations, not hearing her. It was as if she
had said nothing, almost as if she were a creature of his
imagination. It made her nervous.

Nevertheless, the two continued talking idly to one
another while they fished, with long periods of thoughtful
silence between exchanges, and after a while, she no longer
noticed that the other blacks were watching her in attentive
silence whenever he spoke to her, switching off and ignoring
her altogether whenever she responded. Then, in less than
an hour, the afternoon tide turned, and they both finally
started catching fish—spots, small, silvery-white fish with a
thumbnail-sized black dot over each gill.

"The tide comin' in now," he explained. "We goin' t'
get us a mess of fish now, you wait," he said, and as he spoke,
she felt the deliberate tug of a fish on her line. She yanked
with her left hand and reeled with her right, swiftly pulling
in a small fish that glistened in the sun as she drew it up to
the pier and over the rail. The fish she caught, one after
another, were only a bit larger than her hand, but as the man
explained, they'd be the best little fish she'd ever caught.
"You fry up a mess of them little spots in the mo'ning, an'
that'll be your best breakfast!" he promised, excitedly grinning at her as he reeled in another for himself, slipping it off

the hook and stuffing it into the burlap bag at his feet. She
let her own caught fish accumulate inside the tin tackle box
she had brought, her father's. She could hear them rattling
around inside it, scattering the hooks, sinkers and lures in the
darkness. Her heart was pounding, from the work as much
as from the excitement; she imagined the large, grey blossoms
of sweat that she knew had spread across her back and under
her arms. Her arms and legs were feathery and full of light
to her, as, one after another, she felt the shudder and the
familiar, hard tug of a fish hitting the line, and hooked, felt
it pull against the steady draw of the reel. She wanted to
laugh out loud, to yell to the man next to her, *Hey*! I got
another one! and *another* one! and *another* one! as they
kept coming with the afternoon tide.

But she said nothing. They both worked steadily now,
in silence, grabbing the flopping, hooked fish off their lines,
jamming fresh worms onto the hooks, reaching over the rail
and casting the lines, underhanded, in long arcs back down
into the water, feeling the weighted hooks hit the water, sink
a foot or two into it, feeling them get hit again, and then
reeling the fish back towards the pier, lifting them free of
the water into the air and drawing them up to the pier and
the rail again, and again, until her arms began to ache, the
muscles of her right hand between thumb and forefinger to
cramp, sweat rolling across her face, and still the fish kept
on hitting the lines. There was a grim, methodical rhythm to
their movements, and they were working together, it seemed,
the slender, tanned woman in the blouse and shorts and blue
tennis shoes and the black man with the enormous head, a
muscular man in a tee shirt and stained khaki trousers and
bare feet that were the color of vanilla ice cream at the
edges, the color of mahogany on the tops.

And then, as suddenly as it had begun, it was over. Her
line drifted slowly to the bottom and lay there, inert, as if
tied to a rock. His line, five feet away from hers, did the
same. The two of them leaned further out and watched,
waiting. But nothing happened. The fish were gone. The
tide had moved them closer to the beach, where the school
had swirled and dispersed in several silvery clouds, swimming
with the current along the beach, away from the pier and

parallel to the breaking waves. She watched as the
surf-casters scattered up the beach one by one began
catching fish, their long poles going up like toll gates
as the schools of fish moved rapidly along.

She lay flat on her back in the sand, no blanket or
towel beneath her, feeling her skin slowly darken, tiny,
golden beads of sweat gradually stringing her mouth
along her upper lip and over her chin, crossing her forehead just above her eyebrows, puddling in the gullies
below her collarbones and ribcage, between her small
breasts, and drifting, sliding in a thin, slick sheet of
moisture down the smooth insides of her thighs. It
was close to noon, and the sun, a flat, white disc, was
now almost directly overhead, casting practically no
shadow.

"Mommy, you're really getting red," Laura quietly said.
She stood over her mother for a moment, peering down with
a serious, almost worried look on her face. She was the older
daughter, tempermentally more serious than her sister, her
range of emotions normally running from anxiety to grave
concern to anger. They had always called her Laura, had
never tried giving her a nickname. The other child, even
though they'd named her Eva, was called Bootsie, Bunny,
Noosh and Pickle—depending on the parent's mood and the
expression on the face of the child. Eva's range of emotions
seemed normally to run from giddiness to delight to whimsy;
even when she was sobbing, her face red and wet with tears,
it was close to the whimsy end of the spectrum, just as, when
Laura was laughing, it was very close to anxiety. Most people
found the two girls attractive and likeable—as much because
of their personality differences as for their physical simi-
larities, for the four year old Eva was in appearance a smaller
version of the seven year old Laura. And both girls looked
exactly like their mother.

This morning the three of them wore deep purple, two-
piece bathing suits, and while the mother sunbathed, the
daughters, with their pails and shovels, played in the hot
sand beside her. The grandmother had driven into the village
for groceries and mail, and the grandfather had taken his

regular morning walk up the beach to the old Coast Guard
station, a three mile walk.

"Look, Mommy, *sharks!*" Laura cried. Janet propped
herself up on her elbows and squinted against the hard glare
of white sand and mirror-like water. Then she saw them.
Porpoises. Their grey backs slashed in and out of the water
like dark knives chopping across the horizon just beneath the
surface of the water.

"They're not sharks, they're porpoises, Laura."

"Oh. Are they dangerous?"

"Not really. They're supposed to be very bright and
actually friendly."

"Oh," she said, not believing.

Janet lay down on her back again and closed her eyes.
She studied the backs of her eyelids, a yellow ochre sheet
with a slight, almost translucent scratch, like a thin scar, in
front of the lid, between her eyeball and the lid. Every time
she tried to look at the scar—which seemed to float across the
surface, moving slowly, like a twisted reed floating on still
water—it jumped and disappeared off the edge of her circle
of vision. It's probably a tiny scratch on the retina, she
decided. The only way she could actually see it was if she
tried not to look directly at it, but merely looked past it, as
if at something else located in the same general region. Even
then, however, she would find herself eager to see the line
(the scar or scratch or whatever it was), and she would search
for it, would catch a glimpse of it, and chasing with her gaze,
would see it race ahead of her and out of sight.

She realized that the girls were no longer close beside her,
and opening her eyes, sat up and looked around for them.
They were gone. A small flock of gulls loped over the water,
dipping, dropping, lifting, going on. The porpoises were still
looping through the water a few hundred yards from the
beach. The beach, however, as far as she could see in both
directions, was deserted. She called, "Laura!" Then called
again, louder, and stood up, looking back towards the cottage.
Where the hell . . .?

"Listen, Mommy, you're really getting a terrible sunburn!"
She opened her eyes and looked into Laura's worried face.
Eva was sitting a few yards away, humming to herself while

she buried her feet in a knee-deep hole she had dug in the
sand. "Did you fall asleep?" Laura asked.

"No." She stood up then, brushing the sand off the
backs of her slender legs, shoulders and arms. "C'mon, let's
walk up the beach and meet Grandpa," she said cheerfully,
reaching a hand to Laura, leaning down and helping Eva
pull herself free. The three of them started walking down
the beach towards the Coast Guard station. Offshore, the
porpoises cruised alongside, headed in the same direction,
and above them, the gulls.

The third night in the cottage, listening to the radio, a
top-40 station from Elizabeth City, Janet drank alone until
after midnight. She situated herself on the screened porch,
gazed out at the ridge of sand that lay between the cottage
and the beach, milky-white until almost ten o'clock, when it
slowly turned grey, then black, against the deep blue, eastern,
night sky beyond. She was drinking scotch and water, and
each new drink contained less water and proportionately
more scotch than the previous one, until she had succeeded
in blurring her vision, with her face a heavy plaster mask
slipping forward and about to fall into her lap.

She was alone. Her mother and father had done their
drinking before dinner, as was their habit, and had gone to
bed by nine-thirty, which also was a habit. Janet, who had
almost forgotten their routines, had been repelled, and a
flood of sour memories had swept over her, depressing her,
separating her from her own life sufficiently to make her
feel, at last, self-righteous sitting there on the porch with
the bottle of Teacher's, a pitcher of water, a tub of ice cubes,
and a small transistor radio on the floor beside her, pouring
and drinking down one glassful of scotch and water after
another, letting the sweetly sad songs from that summer's
crop swarm over her own self-pitying sense of past and
present lives. At one point she told herself that she was very
interested in the differences between the way her parents
drank and the way she drank—meaning that she was interested
in making sure that there were differences.

As the land behind her cooled, the wind blew steadily
and strongly, and the sound of the waves crashing in dark-

ness on the packed, wet sand filled all the space that lay behind the sound of the radio. Janet thought in clumsy spirals,
about Roger, his years in graduate school, and about their
townhouse in Cambridge, the years before that, when they
both were in college, when the children were born, her preg-
nancies, then the years endured while in high school in Connecticut, living at home with her parents, the summers at
camps in upstate New York, traveling in the West, then a
small girl, visiting her grandparents, here, at Kitty Hawk,
where the family had been coming for their summers for as
long as she could remember . . . and now here she was again,
where she had started, where they had started too, her
parents, and she was placing her own daughters right where
she had been placed, even to the point of sleeping them in
the same room she had used at their age. She felt her chest
and throat fill with a hard fist of longing, a knot of emotion
attached to no object outside herself. Then, almost as soon
as she had become aware of its presence, she felt the knot
loosen and quickly unravel, to regather as hatred, clear anger
and revulsion for her own life, for the entrapment it offered
her. Momentarily satisfied, though, with this object for her
emotion and with the longing converted to anger, she flicked
off the radio, stood clumsily, slightly off-balance, rocking on
the balls of her feet like a losing prize-fighter, and wound her
way back into the livingroom, bumping curtly against the
maple arm of the couch, grabbing at the light switches, dump-
ing the house finally into darkness, as she made her way
down the hall to the stairs and up the stairs to her bedroom,
the "guestroom" at the end, moving with pugnacious con-
fidence in spite of the darkness, but, because of her drunked-
ness, off-balance, inept.

Over on the western side of the Outer Banks, the soundside, the water was shallow and, most of the time, calm. Excellent places for wading lay scattered all along the soundside
north of Kitty Hawk, north to where, standing on any slight
height of land, one could easily see both the Atlantic and
Currituck Sound. The fourth morning at Kitty Hawk, Janet
decided to drive over to the sound and take the girls to one
of the small inlets where they could wade and even swim

safely. They were excited by the prospect, though they didn't quite understand how, only a few miles away, it could be so different. If here by the cottage there was an ocean with huge dangerous waves and undertows and tides, how could they get into the car and go to the water a few miles away and have it be utterly different, like a shallow lake only with salt water?

Driving fast along the narrow road north of Kitty Hawk, deep sand on both sides, witch grass, sea oats and short brush, with high dunes blocking any possible views of the ocean, Janet slowed suddenly and carefully pulled her father's green Chrysler stationwagon over and picked up a hitchhiker. He was slight and not very tall, an inch or two taller than Janet, probably. About twenty-two or -three, with long blond hair, almost white, that hung straight down his back, he moved with an odd, precise care, as if he were made of glass, that was slightly effeminate and, to Janet, extremely attractive. As he came up beside the car he smiled, showing even, white teeth, good-humored blue eyes, a narrow nose. He pitched his backpack into the rear of the car, where the girls were, nodded hello to them and climbed into the front seat next to Janet.

"How far you goin'?" he asked in a soft, confident voice.

"Out beyond Duck, to the sound. Four or five miles, I guess. Will that get you to where you want?"

"Yeah," he answered, sliding down in the seat, folding his hands across his flat belly and closing his eyes, obviously enjoying the smooth luxury of the car, the insulating comfort of the air conditioner, as Janet drove the huge vehicle swiftly along the road, floating over bumps, gliding flatly around curves and bends in the road.

"Connecticut plates," the young man said suddenly, as if remembering a name he'd forgotten. "Are you from Connecticut?" He was unshaven, but his cheeks weren't really bearded as much as merely covered with a soft, blond down. He was well-tanned, dressed in levis, patched and torn, faded and as soft-looking as chamois, and a dark green tee shirt. He was barefoot. Sliding a bit further down on the seat, his weight resting on the middle of his back, he placed his feet onto the dashboard in front of him, gingerly, with a grace and care that made it seem natural to Janet.

She explained that she was from Cambridge, that the car
was her father's and her parents were the ones who lived in
Connecticut. Manchester, outside Hartford. And she was just
down here for a while, she and her daughters, visiting them
at their cottage. Though she herself hadn't been down here
in years, not since her childhood. Because of summer camps
and school and all. . . .

"Yeah, right," he said, peering casually around him,
taking in the two little girls in the back, who grinned sound-
lessly at him, the styrofoam floats in the far back of the car,
beach towels, a change of clothes for each of them, a bag
with sandwiches and cookies in it, a small styrofoam ice
chest with ice and a six-pack of Coke inside. "You going
swimming in the sound?" he asked.

"Yes, for the kids, y' know?" She started to explain,
about the waves, the undertow, the tides, how these presented
no problems over on the sound and children their ages could
actually swim and enjoy themselves, not just sit there digging
in the sand, which was about all they could do over on the
sea side, when she realized that she was talking too much,
too rapidly, about things that didn't matter. So she asked
him, "What about you? Are you staying down here for the
summer . . . or what?"

"No. I'm just kind of passing through. Though I may
stay on for the summer," he added softly. His accent identi-
fied him as a northerner, but that was about all.

"Are you living here . . . in Kitty Hawk, I mean?"

"Naw, I made a camp out on the dunes, a ways beyond
where the road ends. It's a fine place, so long as they don't
come along and move me out. Nobody's supposed to be
like camping out there, you know?"

"Do you have a tent?" she asked, curious.

"No. They'd spot that as soon as I pitched it. I just sort
of leaned some old boards and stuff together, pieces of wood
I found along the beach and in the dunes. Last night, when
it rained, I bet I stayed as dry as you did. It's the best place
I've had all year. Up north, even in summer, there's no way
you can be comfortable, drifting around like this. But like
down here, it's easy, at least till winter comes. I work a couple
of days every couple of weeks pumping gas at the Gulf station
in Manteo, for groceries and stuff, you know? . . . That's

where I'm comin' from now, I got my two weeks' groceries
an' stuff in my pack . . . and I just spend the rest of my time,
you know, out on the dunes, sitting around in my shack,
playing a little music, smoking some good dope, fishing on
the beach . . . stuff like that."

"Oh," she said, surprised to hear herself saying it sharply,
as if he had said something to make her angry.

The road ahead was narrower, and on both sides, dunes
and beach beyond dunes, no vegetation but brown grasses
scattered sparsely across the sands, and as they rounded a
curve, the road ended altogether. There was a paved cul-de-
sac at the end where, without much trouble, one could turn
a car around, and Janet steered the big Chrysler into this
area and parked it, shutting off the motor, opening the door
and stepping out quickly.

The young man got out and walked around to the back,
where he flopped the tailgate down, pulling his pack out
first, then the kids' styrofoam floats, the lunch bag and ice
chest, and the towels and clothes. The girls scrambled past
him, leaped down from the tailgate and ran for the water.
They were already in their bathing suits, and they didn't
break stride as they hit the quietly lapping water and raced
in, quickly finding themselves twenty or thirty feet from
shore, with the water not yet up to their knees. Janet had
come around to the back to get their things out of the car,
but when she got there the man had already placed them on
the ground and was closing the tailgate, lifting it slowly.
Smiling gratefully, she came and stood beside him, to help
lift the massive, heavy tailgate, brushing his bare arm with
hers, then moving tightly towards him, touching his thigh
with the side of her own. Lifting the slab of metal together,
slamming it shut, they moved quickly away from the car
and from each other. She peered easily into his face, and he
answered with a slight smile.

"Want to come up and see my shack?" he asked her. He
stood about eight feet away from her, one hand resting on
his pack.

"Where is it?" she asked him, tossing her head, slinging
a wisp of hair away from her eyes for a second. She leaned
over and picked up the two coffin-shaped floats, hating.

the touch of the things against her hands, their odd weight-lessness.

He waved a hand towards the seaside and said, "A couple hundred yards over that way. Just walk over those dunes there and when you get to the beach go along for maybe a hundred yards and cut in toward the dunes again, and then you'll see my shack. It'll probably look like a pile of driftwood or something to you at first, but when you get closer you'll see that it's a pretty fine place to live," he said, showing his excellent teeth again. "I got some good smoke too, if you care for that."

She looked down at the clothes, the paper bag and ice chest, the beach towels, lying in the sand, then back at the boney youth in front of her.

"Well, no . . . I don't think so. I have my daughters here. They haven't had a chance to swim, really, not since we got here, and I promised them this would be it, a whole day of it. But thanks," she said.

He answered, "Sure," lifted his pack onto his back, jabbing his arms through the straps, turned and started off across the pale sand through slowly waving lines of sea oats, leaving deep, drooping tracks behind him.

She stood at the back of the car for a few moments, watching him depart, then turned and dragged the styrofoam floats down to the edge of the water, where her daughters were waiting for her.

"You coming in too, Mamma?" Eva asked her.

"Yeah, Pickle, I'm coming in too."

"What were you talking about, you and that man?" Laura wondered, looking anxious. She stood knee-deep in the tepid water, about twenty feet from shore.

"Nothing much, really. He wanted me to come and see the way he lived, I guess. He's proud of the way he lives. Some people are that way. You know, proud of the way they live. I guess he's one."

"Are you?" Laura asked without hesitation.

"No," her mother answered, just as swiftly. Then she went back to the car for the rest of their gear.

When she woke the next morning, the first thing she knew was that it was raining—a soft, windless, warm rain, falling in a golden half-light, and she couldn't decide if it had just begun or was about to end.

Dressing quickly, shoving a brush through her hair, she walked out to the hall, heard her daughters talking behind the door of their bedroom, saw that the door to her parents' room was still closed, and judging it to be early, probably not seven yet, walked downstairs to the livingroom. Immediately, upon entering the room, she felt the dampness of it. In the mornings here, the livingroom and kitchen seemed strangely inappropriate to her—wet, chilled, smelling of last night's cigarette butts and food—which made her eager to get a pot of coffee made, bacon frying, ashtrays emptied, the new day begun.

As she moved about the small kitchen, from the formica-topped counter to the stove to the refrigerator, she gradually realized that the rain had stopped, but the golden, hazey light had been replaced by a low, overcast sky casting a field of gloomy, pearly light. She stopped work and looked out the window towards the ocean. A gull, as it swept up from the beach, ascending at the ridge between the cottage and the water, seemed to burst out of the ground. She could see that its belly was stained with yellow streaks the color of egg yolk, and at once she knew that the birds she had believed so pure and cleanly white were actually scavengers, carrion-eaters, foul-smelling, filthy creatures that were beautiful only when seen from a distance, only when abstracted from their own reality. Then suddenly the force of the day, the utter redundancy of it, the closure it represented and sustained, hit her, and she knew she'd been staggered by the blow. She was unwilling to believe that her life was going to be this way every day, unwilling to believe it and yet also unable to deny it any longer—a lifetime of waking to damp, smelly couches and chairs, to rooms filled with furniture in a house, to food again, for herself, for her children, to emptying the ashtrays, and smoking cigarettes to fill them up again, of waking to sodden grey skies and stinking birds searching for garbage, and on through the day, more meals, more messes to make and clean up afterwards, until nightfall, when, with pills or alcohol, she would put her body to sleep for eight or ten hours, to begin it all over again the next morning. It

wasn't that she believed there was nothing more than this.
Rather, she now understood that—no matter what else there
was—she would never get away from this. It was as close to
her as her own body, and therefore, anything else was little
more than worthless. Anything she might successfully add to
her life could only come in as background to this repeated
series of acts, tasks, perceptions, services. She was thirty years
old, not old, and yet it was too late to begin anything truly
freshly. A new man, a new place to live, a new way of life, a pro-
fession even—the newness would be a mockery, a sad, lame reaction to the failure of the old. There had been the last promise,
when she had left Roger, of sloughing off her old life, the way
a snake sloughs off an old skin, revealing a new, lucid, sharply
defined skin beneath it. But the analogy hadn't held.

It occurred to her that she was trapping her own children.
The terms of her life had become the terms of their lives now,
and thus they too would spend the rest of their lives in re-
lentness, unchanging reaction to patterns she could not stop
establishing for them. None of them, not she, not her
daughters, were going to get free. Again, she'd been fooled
again, but this time, she knew, it was for the last time. She
felt a dry bitterness working down her throat, like a wafer
eaten at communion. Walking to the bottom of the stairs, she
quietly called her daughters down for breakfast.

"Look, it's going to be a lousy day all day, so rather than
wait around here hoping the sun will come out, is it okay if
I take your car and spend the day with the kids, driving
around and taking in the sights?" She lit a cigarette, flicked
the match onto the floor, saw it lying there, a thin tail of
smoke ascending from one end, and quickly plucked it back,
wondering what the hell made her do that? She held the
burnt match carefully between her thumb and forefinger
while her father tried to answer her first question.

It was difficult for him, mainly because he wanted her to
know, on the one hand, that he was eager for her to use his
car, that, in fact, he was eager to be able to help her in any
way possible (going for his wallet as the thought struck him),
but also, he wanted her to know that he and her mother

would be forced to endure their day-long absence as a painful
event—wanted her to know this, but didn't want that knowledge to coerce her into changing her mind and staying at the
cottage or leaving the children here while she took the car
and went sight-seeing alone. After all, he reasoned with himself, they were *her* children, and right now they must seem
extra-precious to her, for, without Roger, she must need to
turn to them for even more love and companionship than ever
before. He imagined how it would have been for Anne, his
wife, if they had gotten divorced that time, years back, when
Janet was not much older than Laura was now. Yes, but what
would this day be like for him and for Anne, with Janet and
the children gone? A grey blanket of dread fell across his
shoulders as he realized that five minutes after the car pulled
away, he and his wife would sit down, each of them holding
a book, and they would wait impatiently for the sound of
the car returning. After lunch, they would take a walk up
the beach (if it didn't rain) walking back quickly so as not
to miss them if Janet and the children decided to return to
the cottage early, and, because, of course, they would not
have come back early, he and Anne would spend the rest of
the afternoon in their chairs on the porch, holding their
books, he a murder mystery, she a study of open classrooms
in ghetto schools. Well, they could drink early, and maybe
Anne could think of something special to fix for dinner,
blue shell crabs, and could start to work on that early, and
he could rake the beach again, digging a pit for the trash he
found, burying it, raking over the top of the pit carefully,
removing even the marks left by the teeth of the rake. . . .
    "*Sure* you can take the car, that's a *fine* idea! Give us a
chance to take care of some things around here that need
taking care of anyhow. How're you fixed for cash? Need a
few dollars?" he asked without looking at her, drawing out
his billfold, removing three twenties, folding them with his
second finger and thumb and shoving them at her in such a
way that for her to unfold and count it would be to appear
slightly ungrateful. She could only accept.
    Which she did, saying thanks and going directly into the
livingroom, switching off the television as she told her
daughters to hurry up and get dressed, they were going out

for a ride, to see some exciting things, the Wright Brothers
Memorial, for one thing, and maybe a shipwreck, and some
fishing boats and a lighthouse, and who knows what else.
She looked down at her hand, found that she was still holding
onto the burnt match. She threw it into an ashtray on the
endtable next to the couch.

She drove fast, through the village of Kitty Hawk—several
rows of cottages on stilts, a few grocery stores and filling
stations, a restaurant, a book store, and the Fish Pier—and
south along Highway 158 a few miles, to Kill Devil Hills. The
overcast sky had started breaking into shreds of dirty-grey
clouds exposing deep blue sky behind. Though the day was
warm, the sun was still behind clouds, and thus the light was
cold, diminishing colors and softening the edges of things,
making it seem cooler than it was. Switching the air conditioner off, Janet pressed toggles next to her and lowered
the windows opposite and beside her, and surprisingly warm,
humid air rushed into the car. In the back, the girls had taken
up their usual posts, peering out the rear window, finding it
more satisfying to see where they had been than to seek
vainly for where they were going.
On her right, in the southwest, Kill Devil Hill appeared,
a grassy lump prominent against the flattened landscape of
the Outer Banks, and at the top of the hill, a stone pylon
that, from this distance of a mile, resembled a castle tower.
"We're almost there," she called to the girls. "Look!"
She pointed at the hill and the tower.
"Where?" Laura asked. "Where are we going?"
"There. See that hill and the tower on top? Actually, it's
not a tower. It's a stone memorial to the Wright Brothers,"
she explained, knowing then why she had never come here
before, and simultaneously, wondering why the hell she was
coming here now.
"The Wright Brothers?" Laura said. "Are they the air-
plane men?"
Eva saw the hill and the memorial and exclaimed ex-
citedly that it was a castle.
"Yes, they're the men who invented the airplane."
"Oh."

"Mamma, look! A castle! Are we going to the castle? Can we go to the castle?"

"Yes."

"How many brothers were there?"

"Two. Wilbur and Orville."

"Only *two*? I thought there was *twelve*," Laura cried as if she'd been deceived.

"Will there be a king and a queen at the castle?"

"No . . . yes. Sure."

"Oh, boy! Laura, there's going to be a king and a queen at the castle!"

"Stupid! That's not a castle."

"Yes, it is. Let her call it a castle, Laura. It looks like one."

Off the highway now, they drove along the narrow, winding approach to the memorial, passing the field and the low, flat-roofed, glass-walled structure that, she could see from the roadway, housed the various exhibits and the scale model of the aircraft, past the two wooden structures at the northern end of the field where, she remembered reading once years ago, on an earlier visit, the brothers had housed their device and had worked and slept while preparing it for flight. Janet was surprised to find herself oddly attracted to the place, the hill, round and symmetrical, like an Indian mound, topped with the pylon that even up close looked like a castle, the way, as a child, she had imagined the Tower of London to look, and spreading below it, the flat, grass-covered field with the grey structures, like small garages or barns, at the far end.

Janet parked the Chrysler over on the west side of the hill where there was a small parking lot. The three of them got out and started walking quickly along the asphalt paved pathway that methodically switchbacked to the top. In seconds, the girls had run on ahead, and Janet was alone. The sky was almost clear now, a bright, luminous blue, and the sun was shining down on her face as she climbed. She was sweating and enjoying it, feeling the muscles of her back and legs working hard for the first time in weeks. The closure she had felt a few hours ago she could now recall only with deliberate effort. She still perceived the entrapment as the prime fact of her life, but merely as if it were a statistic, as impersonal as her shoe size. Ahead of her, the figures of her daughters were darting about the base of the tower, peering up at the top, scurrying around the thing as if looking for an entrance. Then, in a few moments, she, too, arrived at the crest, breathing hard, sweating, and the girls ran to meet her.

"It's a castle all right!" Eva cried happily. "But we can't get in, the door's locked!" She pulled Janet by the hand, to show her that in fact there was an entrance to the tower, the castle—a steel door that was padlocked. "The king and the queen had to go to work, I guess. They aren't home."

"I guess not, Pickle," Janet said, walking slowly around to the other side, sitting on the ground and peering down at the slope the two bicycle mechanics had used for flying their strange machine. Then, as if a wonder were unfolding before her eyes, filling her with awe, she saw a large, clear image of the two men from the midwest, their clumsy wire, wood and cloth aircraft, the sustained passion, the obsession, which was the work, their love for it and for each other. It was like discovering a room in her own house that she never before had suspected even existed, opening a door that she'd never before opened, looking in and seeing an entire room, unused, unknown, altering thoroughly and from then on her view of the entire house.

The image, of course, was of her own making, but that made no difference to her, did not lessen the impact at all. She saw the brothers as having released into their two individual lives tremendous energy, saw it proceeding directly, as if from a battery, from the shared obsession and the mad, exclusive love for each other—a positive and a negative post, the one necessitated by the presence of the other. They did not permit themselves (she decided) to live as she had feared she was condemned to live—curled up inside a self that did not really exist, slowly dying inside that shell, no matter how many additional whorls of shell she managed to extrude, each new whorl no more than a dumb reaction to the limits of the previous one, spun by anger or bitterness or despair.

For her, the perception of the image was experienced by her body as much as by her mind, and she felt astonishingly lightened by it, as if she could fly, like a deliberately wonderful bird, leaping from the lip at the top of the little hill, soaring from that height of land first up and then out, in a long, powerful glide across the downward slope and then over the field that aproned it, drifting easily, gracefully, slowly down to the ground, coming to rest at the far end of the field, where the two workshops were located, where, she decided, she would go to work, pitching herself into the task of making a machine that could fly, making it out of wires and shreds of cloth and odd remainders of wood and rough pieces of other machinery—the junk of her life so far. Her daughters careened past her, mocking and singing at each other, asserting their differences to each other, and she knew, from the way her face felt, that she would be tireless.

Standing, she turned and waved for the girls to follow, and the three of them descended the hill, holding hands and talking brilliantly.

THE NEIGHBOR

The idea was to watch his gaunt wife, seated on the sulky, drive the chocolate colored mare down the dirt road to the general store, to make a small purchase there, and return. He was a black man in his fifties, she a white woman the same age, his children (from a previous marriage) were black, her children (also from a previous marriage) were white. Everyone else in town was white also. Many of them had never seen a black man before this one. That's probably why he had this idea about the sulky and his wife and the store.

On the other hand, he may have had it because he and his wife and all their children were incompetent and, in various ways, a little mad. The madness had got them kicked out of the city, but here, after three years in this small, farm community north of the city, it was the incompetence that angered the people around them. Country people can forgive madness, but a week ago, the family's one immediate neighbor, a dour young man in his late twenties, had walked out his back door and had seen, for the tenth time, one of their chickens scratching in his pathway to the woodpile. He'd rushed back into his house, and returning with an Army .45 handgun, had fired eight bullets into the chicken, making a feathered, bloody mess of it.

That night, the black man with his two teenaged daughters and his two teenaged stepsons and his wife drove to the racetrack and bought for one hundred dollars an unclaimed, chocolate colored trotter, an eighteen year old mare named Jenny Lind. They rented a van and lugged her home and put her in the barn with the goats, sheep, chickens, and the two Jersey heifers. The farm, the huge barn, the animals—except for the mare—were all part of an earlier idea, the idea

of living off the land. But the climate had proved harsh, the
ground stoney and in hills, the neighbors more or less un-
cooperative—and of course there was that incompetence.

It was the end of the summer, and every morning as the
sun rose the black man got up and before his breakfast walked
the mare along the side of the dirt road in the low, cold mist.
Behind him, in layers, were the brown meadow, the clumpy
rows of gold and ruby colored elm trees, and the dark hills
and the mist-dimmed, orange sun. Every morning he paraded
Jenny Lind the length of the route he had planned for his
wife and the sulky—his jet black arm raised to the bridle, his
face proudly looking straight ahead of him as he walked past
his neighbor's house, his mind reeling with delight as he
imagined his wife in her frail-wheeled sulky riding to the
store, where she would buy him some pipe tobacco and
some salt for the table, a small package to be wrapped in
brown paper and tied with string, and then returning along
the curving dirt road to the house, one of her sons or his
daughters would run out, and holding the reins for her,
would help her step graciously down. In that way, the horse
received its daily exercise—for no one in the family knew
how to ride, because, as he insisted, no one in the family had
been to a riding academy yet, and besides, Jenny Lind was a
trotter.

They searched all over the state for a sulky they could
afford, but no one would sell it to them. Finally, he phoned
the man at the race track who had sold them the horse and
learned of a good, used sulky for sale in a town in the far
southwest corner of the state. That morning, after exercising
the mare, he and his wife got into the pickup truck and drove
off to see about the used sulky.

All day long, the two teenaged sons and the two teenaged daughters rode the mare, bareback, up and down the
dirt road, galloping past the neighbor's house, braking to a
theatrical stop at the general store, and galloping back again.
A hundred times they rode the old horse full-speed along
that half-mile route. Silvery waves of sweat covered her
heaving sides and neck, and her large, watery eyes bulged from
the exertion, and late in the afternoon, as the sun was drifting quickly down behind the pines in back of the house, the

mare suddenly veered off the road and collapsed on the front
lawn of the neighbor's house and died there. The boy who
was riding her was able to leap free of the collapsing bulk,
and astonished, terrified, he and his brother and stepsisters
ran for their own house and hid in a loft over the barn, where,
eating sandwiches and listening to a transistor radio, they
awaited the return of their parents.

The neighbor stood in his livingroom and as darkness
came on stared unbelieving at the dead horse on his lawn.
Finally, when it was completely dark and he couldn't see it
anymore, he went out onto his front porch and waited for
the black man and his wife to come home.

Around ten o'clock, he heard their pickup clattering
along the road. The truck stopped beside the enormous bulk
of the horse. With the pale light from the truck splashed
across its dark body, the animal seemed of gigantic propor-
tions, a huge, equestrian monument pulled down by vandals.
The neighbor left his porch and walked down to where the
horse lay. The black man and his wife had got out of their
truck and were sitting on the ground, stroking the mare's
forehead.

The neighbor was a young man, and while a dead animal
was nothing new to him, the sight of a grown man with black
skin, weeping, and a white woman sitting next to him, also
weeping, both of them slowly stroking the cold nose of a
horse ridden to death—that was something he'd never seen
before. He patted the woman and the man on their heads,
and in a low voice told them how the horse had died. He was
able to tell it without judging the children who had killed
the animal. Then he suggested that they go on to their own
house and he would take a chain and with his tractor would
drag the carcass across the road from his lawn to their
meadow, where tomorrow they could bury it by digging a
pit next to it, close enough, he told them, so that all they
would have to do was shove the carcass with a tractor or a
pickup truck and it would drop in. They quietly thanked
him and got up and climbed back into their truck and drove
to their own house.

THE LIE

A ten year old boy—maybe eleven maybe nine but no older
and certainly no younger—kills his buddy one Alfred Coburn
while the two are enemy espionage agents engaged in a life-or-
death struggle in the middle of the wide perfectly flat tarred
roof of an American owned hotel in Hong Kong. The young
killer whose name is Nicholas Leburn stabs his good buddy
in the chest just below the left nipple slicing deftly between
two ribs thence through the taut pericardium and plunging
unimpeded into the left ventricle of the heart—stabs his
friend with an inexpensive penknife manufactured by the
Barlow Cutlery Corp., of Springfield, Massachusetts. This
knife has a plastic simulated wood grip and a 2-1/2" steel
blade. Also a 1-1/2" smaller narrower blade.

Alfred poor wide-eyed Alfred squeaks in surprise and falls,
Nicholas understands what has happened and runs home.
    A distance of approximately one city block separates the
Transilex parking lot that has been serving as the roof of an
American owned hotel in Hong Kong and the asbestos
shingled wood-framed mid-Victorian house that has been
serving as the Lebrun home and hearth for over forty years—
ever since Nicholas' paternal grandfather was a young newly
wedded still childless man. Nicholas' grandfather was named
Ernest but he was called Red because of the color of his
thick short-cropped hair and moustache. A clock maker and
a good one too Ernest learned his trade (he would have said
craft) in his home town of Hartford, Connecticut, and then
emigrating to Waltham, Massachusetts, when the time in-
dustry shifted to that city shortly before the outbreak of
World War II, he went to work for the Waltham Watch

Company. A French Protestant and native New Englander, Ernest Lebrun: thrifty, prudent, implacably stable, high-minded and honorable, incorruptible, intelligent, organized, good-humored—all resulting in his having become well-liked and financially secure well before he was forty years old. It might be told that he died in a dreamless sleep shortly after World War II had finally ground to a bewildered halt and sometime during the year that commenced with his grandson Nicholas' birth and winked out with the child's first birthday, a fact surely of considerable moment for Ernest (Red): hanging onto shreds of life until after the birth of his first male grandchild the son of an only son assured finally and at the very end of the continuation of the name, etc.

It is because of the distance between the Transilex parking lot and home and because he ran all the way home that Nicholas is out of breath panting and redfaced when he turns into the scrubby yard and thus arrives safely at what appears to be and what later turns out to be heaven.

Robert Lebrun the boy's middle-ageing auburn haired father a paid-in-full member of the United Association of Plumbers and Pipefitters (AFL-CIO) Local #143 is comfortably swinging on the porch glider smoking an after-supper cigar in the orange summer evening light and from time to time reading from the tabloid newspaper spread on his lap.

Abruptly Nicholas parks himself next to his father upsetting with his momentum the glider's gentle vacillation and the father asks the son his only child heir to his ancient name and lands why is he running? The lad tells his father why he is running. Not of course without considerable encouragement from the father—whose cigar goes slowly out during the telling.

Young Nicholas does not forget to mention the fact that just as he steps off the flat square expanse of tar that has been serving as the Transilex parking lot—now almost innocent of parked automobiles—and onto Brown Street's narrow sidewalk he happens to glance back at his little friend's fallen body, that small heap of summer clothing and inert flesh already used-up and thrown out dropped in the middle

of the great black square. A little crumpled pile of stuff lying
next to the front tire of a bottle-green British Ford sedan.
And in that fraction of a second Nicholas realizes that the
owner of the bottle-green sedan—a man who lives in the
neighborhood and who unfortunately is notoriously effeminate a practicing pederast in fact mocked to his face by all
the neighborhood kids and behind his soft back by all the
parents—is strolling blithely across the lot is approaching his
little car from the side opposite Nicholas and the car's right
front tire. . . .

Now it's possible that the man whose name is Toni Scott
does catch a glimpse of Nicholas in flight, but that possibility
shall have to remain equivocal and unrealized. The facts which
follow shall demonstrate why this is so.
    Toni who works as a waiter in an attractively decorated
Boston cocktail lounge of socially ambiguous though not in-
considerable fame for several years now has been saving at
least five dollars a month by parking his car (illegally) in the
Transilex parking lot always taking care to remove his car
well before the nine P. M. departure of the Transilex cafeteria
second shift and—because of his nighttime working hours—
usually managing to slip the innocuous little sedan back into
the lot sometime between the four A. M. unlocking and five
A. M. arrival of the cafeteria first shift. However this particular summer evening ritual removal of his car from its stolen
space definitely even though only partially and from afar *is*
observed over young Nicholas Lebrun's fleeing shoulder
(fateful damning backward glance!) just before the rigorously
bathed meticulously groomed idly smiling Toni Scott filled
to the eyes with sweet memories and still sweeter anticipation
discovers Alfred Coburn's hard sunhaired body by accidentally
smashing its rib-cage, sternum and spine with the right front
tire of his bottle-green car.
    He cuts the wheel hard to the left, revs up the tiny four
cylinder motor and spins the car backwards swinging the
front of the car around in an arc to the right—so that he
can make his exit from the lot by the very gate Nicholas has
used just seconds earlier. . . .

It is at this point in the boy's narrative that Robert Lebrun interrupts his son and compels him to insist that no one absolutely no one saw him stab his playmate. He makes the boy reassure him that he (Nicholas) did not extract the pen-knife from Alfred's chest—an unnecessary reassurance for Toni's right front tire has already torn the knife from its nest of flesh, bone and blood, has ground it against pavement, paint, white pebbles in the tar, has smashed the plastic simulated wood grip and removed all fingerprints. Then Lebrun makes Nicholas repeat several times the part of his narrative that has to do with Toni Scott's arrival on the scene and finally after telling his son in clear exact and step-by-step terms just what he intends to do Lebrun stomps into the house and yelling Emergency Police! to the telephone operator he calls the cops.

In a stage-whisper and speaking rapidly he says that he is Robert Lebrun of number forty-eight Brown Street and his son and another neighborhood kid have just been sexually molested by the neighborhood fag and his son broke away from the guy but the other kid is still with the sonofabitch in his car which is parked in the Transilex parking lot the one that used to be the old Waltham Watch factory lot and he (Lebrun) is leaving right now to kill that filthy sonofabitch with his bare hands so if they want Toni Scott alive they have about three minutes to get to him. He makes one other call— to Alfred Coburn senior over on Ash Street some three blocks further from the parking lot than the Lebrun house is—and using that same rapid whispery voice he tells Alfred Coburn senior what he has just related to the cops.

Then Lebrun lunges for the parking lot and Toni Scott who dials the police department from the public phone booth that stands luminous in a dark corner of the lot hears through the glass walls the rising shrieks of approaching sirens before he has even completed dialing the number. . . .

In this story everyone who lies and knows that he lies does so effectively. That is he is believed. Furthermore everyone who lies and yet knows not that he lies—meaning for example Evelyn Lebrun (Nicholas' adoring mother) and poor Alfred

Coburn senior and the two or three neighborhood ladies who
claim they saw Toni Scott talking to the boys from inside
his little green foreign car heard the awful thing call the tykes
from their play saw him smilingly offer them candy if they
would get into his car—these also manage to lie effectively:
they are believed by the police, the rest of the people in the
neighborhood, the newspapers, *Time*, the district attorney,
the psychiatrists testifying for the prosecution, the psychiatrists testifying for the defense, the defense attorney himself
(although he pretends not to believe), the judge, the jury, and
the U.S. Court of Appeals.

Everyone who tells the truth—meaning Toni Scott the
thirty-eight year old fatting balding homosexual—tells the
truth stupidly, inconsistently, alternately forgetting and
remembering critical details, lying about other unrelated
matters, and so on into the night. Toni Scott is not believed
although now and then he probably is pitied. . . .

Thus the compassionately prompt arrival of the police at the
scene of Alfred Coburn's beastly murder—twice-slain savagely
by a scorned and therefore enraged deviate—plucks Toni
Scott from the huge pipe fitter's hands of Robert Lebrun
only to set him down again one year later in Walpole State
Prison (life plus ninety-nine years).

It may have been noticed that the original lie originated with
Nicholas' dad. It was not mentioned however that once the
lie had been designed and manufactured, once it had been
released to the interested public, Robert Lebrun began to
have certain secret misgivings about the way the lie was being
used. The cause of these hesitant shadowy misgivings was
not as one might suppose the absurd fate of Toni Scott.
Rather it was the consummate skill, the unquestioning grace
of movement from blatant truth to absolute falsehood that
consistantly repeatedly and under the most trying of circumstances was demonstrated by Robert Lebrun's only begotten
son the young Nicholas Lebrun. It was almost as if for
Nicholas there was no difference between what actually
happened and what was said to have happened.

"What happened, Nickie?" his father asks. "Why the hell you running in this heat? You never run like that when you're called, only when you're being chased."

"Nobody's chasing me," the kid answers, "but something really awful happened."

"What?"

"I don't know actually. Me and Al was just playing around, see, and he got cut with a knife, only I didn't mean it, it was an accident, honest. You gotta believe me, Pa." The boy uses the same name for his father that Robert Lebrun was taught to use for his.

This probably is the point at which Lebrun begins shuffling fearfully through his memories and imagination for an alibi. The fear of retribution which he now believes to be dominating his son's entire consciousness (even to the boy's physical perceptions, of the scaley white glider, the splintery porch floor catching against the corrugated bottoms of his U. S. Keds, the cooling air laden with the smell of freshly cut grass, the cold zinc-smell of his father's dead cigar, the sounds of his mother's sleek hands washing dishes in warm soapy water)—this fear is in reality now the father's very own.

The father attributes to his son the overwhelming quantity of fear that he knows would have to be his were *he* ten or nine or eleven years old and faced with "something really awful", "an accident", a wounding that occurs without warning, absolute and in its own terms as well. Right in the middle of a game.

The father's now, the force behind the knife as it buries a 2-1/2″ steel blade in the playmate's boney chest; then comes the realization that the boy is dead absolutely and forever no joke no pretense no foolish vain imitation of the absence of existence; his now, the flight from the body's silent accusation away from this gusty hotel rooftop so deserted and stark in the midst of ragged teeming Oriental architecture; and his, the image seen through tinted wraparound glass of the figure of Toni Scott swishing across the lot towards his bottle-green sedan. . . .

And thus Robert Lebrun lies not to save his son but

rather to save himself. His own father Ernest (Red) Lebrun would have found the dynamic reversed from the beginning of the lie to the end, and no doubt Robert at some point along the progression was aware of this, knew that his own father were *he* placed in a similar circumstance would not have been able to credit *his* son with possessing an over-powering fear of retribution and thus the child's experience would have remained intact, still his very own, unmolested by the rush of the father's consciousness of himself. And no doubt this awareness of how Ernest Lebrun would have responded to a similar set of circumstances, circumstances in which he Robert Lebrun would have been the lonely un-molested son, was a critical factor in making it impossible even now for Robert to become anything other than that lonely unmolested son. The red-headed Ernest gave to his young son an absolute truth and an absolute falsity and for that reason Robert was forever a child. Robert to his son gave relative truth and relative falsity and for that reason Nicholas was never a child.

The question of responsibility then seems not to have been raised in at least three generations.

WITH CHÉ AT THE PLAZA

Holding my *Times* unfolded in front of me, now and then glancing up with casual effect, as if deeply engrossed in thought, I carefully looked him over. I did not want him to know that he'd been recognized. Naturally. He was well-groomed, which surprised me at first, but then I quickly understood. Although somewhat longer than that of most latins (but all the more fashionable for it), his dark brown hair was cut in one of those deliberately unkempt, over-the-collar razor-cuts designed by Vidal Sassoon. He still wore a moustache, but a very thin one, carefully trimmed, and he looked barber-shaved. With his bright blue eyes and dark, bronze-tanned skin, he looked rather like a man who'd just spent a month in Jamaica or St. Croix, or maybe one who habitually visited a health club to use the sun lamp. It didn't matter; the effect was the same. All in all, he was very hand-some, especially when you thought of what he must have been through these last few years.

He was wearing, that first morning at the Plaza, an ele-gant, avocado-green, Pierre Cardin jacket and double-knit slacks, muted lemon color, and soft-looking British shoes, an Edwardian cut that since then I've learned is extremely stylish in London and Paris and only just beginning to catch on in New York. He also wore a high-collared, white-on-white shirt with a French foulard necktie that could not possibly have been obtained for less than thirty dollars. He was an extremely *dapper* man, I must say, especially sitting there at breakfast in the Green Tulip Room of the Plaza Hotel. He seemed to be at ease, quite comfortable in such luxurious surroundings, unhesitatingly choosing the correct silver, dealing with the pack of eager waiters so gracefully and unselfconsciously that I almost envied him his élan and overall aura of entitledness, the kind of eclât with which he moved through his moment.

Clearly, it was important to him that he not be recognized. I was almost ashamed for having succeeded where evidently everyone else—probably for the entire five year period since his death was first announced—had failed. What a stroke of genius, though, to hold up at the Plaza! *Naturally* no one would recognize him here, where every guest looks like a celebrity, where everyone has a face that can't help but look slightly familiar. In such a gathering, no one would bother trying to identify exactly the face of Ché Guevara; the mere fact that it was slightly familiar would satisfy. For example, everyone I've seen so far this morning looks like a person from an advertisement in *The New Yorker*. Thus, by eight A. M. I no longer am noticing faces at all unless they are clearly identifiable, like, say, John Wayne's, or unless they are totally anonymous—faces one simply does not see at the Plaza. And it's for that very reason that Ché is safer here than probably anywhere else in the hemisphere. Once he steps outside the Plaza, though, he's in terrible trouble. One hopes the move will never be necessary. If a man has enough money, or his credit holds, he can spend his entire life inside the Plaza and never want for anything. Doubtless that's been Ché's *modus vivendi* for, what, five years now. Incredible! Brilliant, though. You have to hand it to these latin revolutionaries. You really do. Regardless.

He must be lonely, I thought. His contact with the outside world has to be minimal, possibly only through the Cuban delegation to the United Nations. And even at that, he probably has direct contact with only one man there. Ché Guevara, alive and well at the Plaza, would be utterly useless, if not destructive, to the Revolution. Isn't it odd, then, that the only place he really *could* be alive and well is the Plaza? The irony of a life after death is almost enough to make a man question its worth.

He has beautiful eyes. And though they are at moments

tender, brightly humorous, slightly mocking, from the constant steely glint it's clear that this waiting game has ground a sharp edge onto his old, well-known romanticism. It would probably be a pleasure for him if I made myself known to him and we talked awhile on subjects such as the possibilities of justice and autonomy, or the ancient conflict between the needs of society and the needs of the individual, or perhaps death, vanity, love of mankind, hatred of it, or simply nostalgia, melancholy. Over our eggs benedict we could opine in low, vaguely cheerful voices as to how things have been trending in the hemisphere this past decade. I could offer an enthusiasm, a belief, a genuine affection for the future, something he obviously needs these days.

Imagine how the days must go for him! He must be limited to a fairly inflexible routine, and thus his routine cannot be used to speed the day but rather merely to measure it out. Unable to leave the hotel, he breakfasts every morning in the Green Tulip Room, after first having purchased his newspaper in the lobby newsstand. Ordering one of the seven breakfasts listed on the menu, he reads the headlines, quickly grows bored with them. Unlikely to make himself clumsy by unfolding the large sheets of paper to read them at the table, he lets his eyes drift away from the newspaper lying flat on the table before him and studies the struts and buttresses of the cathedral-like interior of the restaurant, admiring them, finding himself recalling a dim cathedral in Buenos Aires, remembering his mother, a slender, aristocratic woman with a tingling laugh and a readiness to weep for the fate of the Argentine peasant, a "Freethinker" who nevertheless went to mass weekly where, because of her social commitment, she prayed for the masses. Her commitment to society, to making it lovable, gave her extraordinary energy and led her confidently to dismiss any petty impulses she might have felt leading her towards consistency.

Here is a letter Ché sent to his mother, in code, of course, sent by way of his man in the Cuban delegation at the U. N. *My dear mother. The days are long for me—I ache with the memory of the ribs of my Rosinant between my heels, my shield upon my arm, my lance tipped towards the future. My nights are long also, filled with dreams of the past. Except*

when I am asleep, I feel myself to have dropped out of time.
That is society's ultimate gift to mankind—she places him
into time, into a history that continues daily to unfold. I
don't believe that in my deepest self I have changed much.
My Marxism has strong roots, as you know, and can live and
even grow with remarkably little tending or water. My youth
was vivid enough to justify a reflective old age, eh? Mostly
what I feel deprived of now is the opportunity to give life an
abrazo, *a hug. I have a friend now, which gives me some*
pleasure and, indeed, even comfort. I find myself looking
forward to our conversations, which are always passionately
abstract. He is an American businessman from one of the
provinces who spends a considerable time in Nueva York
because of his business. It is a successful business, I suppose,
because he always stays at this hotel, which is quite expensive.
He does not know who I am yet, but I think he has guessed
it. So far, I have been guilty of encouraging him to provide
me with what I feel so barren of myself—enthusiasm, a belief
in the future and in the principled lives of men. He has these
(enthusiasm and belief) and I take them from him to nurture
and restore to health my wan and sickly spirit. At times I
think he is one of those strange and frightening American
innocents, like the ones who used to work for the fruit com-
panies. But he is better than that. He is deep, compassionate,
with an imaginative relation to men who happen to be radi-
cally different from him, whether they be peasants or men
like myself. In general, his historical view is an optimistic
one. I don't think he has traveled much. Well, this has gone
on long enough. (My courier will complain if I don't close
here.) I will write you again next month. An abrazo *for you*
from your obstinate and prodigal son. Ernesto.

"You have been living here at the hotel a long time, eh?"
"Sí. Yes ¿And you?"
"¡No, no! I stay here when I am in Nueva York, that's
all. My home is in Massachusetts."
"Ah-h-h. Massa-shoosetts. Yes, I know much of this place,
your home. I have read much of it . . . your transcendental
políticos. How deeply I admire them, Emerson, Thoreau,
Alcott, the woman, what was her name? Fuller, Margaret

Fuller, the one who fought in Italy and died in the shipwreck. Ah, yes, they were extraordinary human beings."
    "Sí."
    "¿And you, are you one of these too?"
    "¿What?"
    "A transcendentalist . . . un hombre que . . . you know,
like Emerson."
    "Ah, well, not exactly, though there is much in Emerson
I agree with and much more that I deeply admire, and I *was*
raised as a Unitarian . . . Still and all, my feet are pretty much
rooted to the ground. This isn't to say that I don't have a
deep commitment to ideals, especially social ideals, no sir.
That's the part of Emerson and Thoreau and all those people
I admire the most. Their social commitment."
    "I see. For them such a commitment, though, was the
consequence of a . . . ¿how shall I say it? . . . a *philosophy*.
For you it is different, ¿no?"
    "Right. For me, what's best for the many is what's best
for society as a whole, and since I am a member of that
society, I stand to benefit in the long run. It's mechanistic,
I know, and self-interest is at the power-drive end of the
chain, but what the hell, I mean, that's fine. It's how society
improves itself."
    "This, then, is a time of decadence, for transcendentalism,
¿no?"
    "Oh yeah, I'd have to say that. Definately."
    "Then there is no need for me to visit Massa-shoosetts."
    "¡God, no! You're as well-off staying here at the Plaza.
Especially if the only thing about Massachusetts that you're
interested in is transcendentalism."
    "It has been a great pleasure talking with you, señor. I
hope we will have an opportunity to chat again during your
brief stay here."
    "Oh, I'm sure we will. And the pleasure was all mine, be-
lieve me, Mr . . . I'm sorry, I didn't catch your name. . . ."
    "¡Oh!"

    Up near his right temple there is a thin, white scar. It
starts at the hairline, jogs down to the earlobe and disappears
behind the ear, like a path disappearing into the jungle. I

didn't notice the scar until the time we were talking intently
of his diminished hopes for an international American revolution, our heads bent forward over the table as we talked, he
staring straight down at the white tablecloth as if into deepest space, his blue eyes glazed over with the dead dream, while
I searched his face, the deep lines across his forehead and
around his eyes, the egocentric, highly intelligent jut of his
brow, nose and chin, searched the details of his face for a
clue to his deepest need, so that I could know what aspect of
that need, if any, I could satisfy, what role I could play in the
final comforting of this savaged hero. That's when I first saw
the scar. It was in a sense . . . beautiful. It looked like the carefully disguised edge of a mask. I broke into one of his melancholy pauses and asked him how he had obtained the scar,
drawing it with my forefinger on my own face, letting my
finger trail off into the thatch of hair below my right ear.

"When you receive a scar such as mine," he told me, "it
is because you have been thought dead and someone wishes
to mutilate the body, or else it is because you are killing
someone and he has proved to be almost capable of stopping
you."

I asked him which it had been for him.

. He said, "Both. They were the same for me."

I am lying asleep in my room at the Plaza. In the dream,
I am alone in the room. The hum of the air conditioner and
the occasional, rising blat of an automobile or bus on the
street below, these are the only sounds. The room lingers in
semidarkness, a grey light, as in the half-hour before dawn or
after sunset, when something momentous is about to begin,
or has just ended. I wake from my dream of a poker game
with Robert Kennedy, Lyndon Johnson, Perry Como and
Frank Sinatra at Sinatra's Palm Beach home. We have been
playing at a round, glass table on the courtyard by the kidney-
shaped pool. An assortment of gorgeous young women in
bikinis lounge around the edge of the pool, and I start to
drift back into that dream, forgetting the portentous atmos-
phere of my hotel room, eagerly dropping into the cardgame,
quiet, lush, tense, at Sinatra's. The five of us—Perry Como,
Robert Kennedy, Lyndon Johnson, Frank Sinatra, and of

course, me—are in bathing suits and dimestore rubber shower
clogs. The bathing suits are slick, black tanksuits. We are
stripped for action. No frills, I think. I remember thinking,
This is really *it*.

Sinatra grins and calls.

Como nonchalantly shrugs and dribbles his five cards
onto the heap of dollars, coins and jewels in the center of the
table. "You got me, boys," he says, grinning helplessly, eyebrows pointing towards the top of his head. "A pair of johnson bars and a pair of trays, jacks, and threes." He pulls a
cigarette from the pack in front of him, Chesterfields, lights
it, inhaling deeply.

Kennedy is scratching his head worridly, every now and
then tossing his hair back with a flick of his head, a nervous,
habitual gesture. Then suddenly, snickering through his nose,
almost embarrassed, it seems, he lays his cards down in front
of him, face-up. "Ah . . . I'm not sure how this'll go with
you fellas . . . but I've got a straight. Foah, five, six, seven,
eight." He giggles and looks sheepishly from one man to the
other, evoking no visible reaction.

Then Johnson snorts like a bull, plopping his cards down.
"Shit! Why don't someone jus' kick my ass when I go off t'
play cards with you fellers? You boys're beatin' my ol'
country ass a goddam mile! 'Course I got me a coupla cards
that're better'n ol' Bobby's, but I can tell that's jus' to suck
me into stayin' in the game so's ol' Frankie can whomp my
ass, ain't that the truth, Frank?" He leers across at Sinatra,
turning over his cards one by one, a straight, king-high. Let
Sinatra beat that sonofabitchin' hand!

Sinatra winks at Como and Kennedy, an obvious stage-
gesture, splays his cards out in a fan, revealing his full house,
three kings and two queens. He reaches for the pot. "Ol'
buddy Lyndon, lemme give it to you straight," he croons.
"Mamma always told me that if I hadda play cards, make
damned sure I play with Irishers and Texans, and always
make sure there's another wop in the game someplace."

That's when I start flipping my four aces onto the table,
one ace at a time—clubs, diamonds, hearts, spades. Shocked,
hurt, the other players silently gape at the cards as they
tumble onto the glass. I reach forward and pull the pile of

money to me and slowly stack it, all the bills in one pile, the
change in another, the jewelry—watches, rings, brooches,
etc.—in a third. I estimate that there's half a million dollars in
the pot.

Johnson and Sinatra stare coldly at me, as if I have somehow cheated. Kennedy and Como look more sorrowful and
personally hurt than angry. They look betrayed. I almost
want to apologize to these two, to explain why I have done
this, but to the others I feel nothing but contempt mixed
with fear. I jam the money and jewelry into a paper sack
and quickly get up from the table. Sinatra, looking up and
slightly behind me, as if someone were hulking behind my
back, says evenly, "Sit down. You're not splitting now,
mister."

I know that if I do not obey, I will be shot in the base
of the skull from six inches away. And that's when I come
ripping away from the dream, locating myself back in my
room at the Plaza. Sitting up in the bed, rubbing my eyes
furiously, still angry and slightly frightened because of the
dream, I realize that I am staring into the solemn face of Ché.
He is seated in the armchair next to the air conditioner,
smoking with exquisite care a long, slender cigar. He has his
beret and Cuban army fatigues on, the first time I've seen
him dressed like this—out of his disguise, as it were.

"Amigo," he says to me in his low, smooth voice, "you
had a close call, ¿eh? Playing games with hombres like those
ones can prove . . . dangerous."

"Yeah."

"¿Are you all right?"

"Sí. Thanks for getting me out of there."

"¿Did you bring it with you?"

"Of course." I reach forward with the paper sack and
place it into Ché's outstretched hand. "I figure it's about
half a million American dollars. Those guys don't play for
peanuts."

"No, muchacho, they don't. And you and I, amigo, we
don't play, as you say, for peanuts either," he says quietly,
almost murmuring the words, drawing a black revolver out
of the bag, aiming it at my chest, pulling the trigger, the room
exploding in smoke, noise, the machismo laughter of Latin
American sadism. . . .

I lay in bed for a long time, my blood racing, my body wet with sweat. I could still hear the occasional beeps of traffic twelve floors below, my own rapid breathing, the low hum of the air conditioner. This Guevara thing was getting out of hand. I was beginning to wish I had never met the man.

Well, I just walked right up to him when he was at breakfast in the Green Tulip Room. He was, as usual, glancing over the headlines of *The Times*, sipping orange juice from a tall, frosty glass, and didn't see me approach him. I pulled out the chair opposite his and sat down quickly, facing him. "Forgive me for interrupting you, Ernesto, but I must speak with you a moment, I hope you'll understand."

"¿Eh? ¿What?" He smiled uneasily, looked around him once, verifying that I was alone.

"There's got to be some way for us to benefit each other, without one or the other of us taking such a terrible loss . . .," I began. Then, looking into his startled eyes, the eyes of a mountain goat suddenly surprised by an unexpected climber, I realized that he had somehow foreseen this moment, as if with his genes, an instinctive kind of anticipation, and thus I realized that there already had been a terrible loss, for me. He would deny everything, I knew, politely disengaging himself from the conversation, looking anxiously for the waiter, pretending that he'd been cornered by a crazy man.

There was nothing else I could do then, or say. "Oh, I'm *terribly* sorry," I tried. "I mistook you for someone else, a friend of mine. I was expecting to meet him here for breakfast. I hope you'll forgive me."

He smiled nervously at me, nodded, and pointedly turned his attention back to the newspaper, as I got up from the chair and fled the dining room for the lobby.

THE MASQUERADE

They were calm, business-like months, as tribute, taxes,
praise and easily met requests rolled in from everywhere, relaxed smiles greeting me on my rounds, making the rounds
seem merely ritualistic, or possibly traditional, ceremonial.
Of course, in a way it was an interregnum, but I had no way
of knowing it then. For the first time in my life, I was
watching my life from above and outside it, and I simply
assumed that the shift, from turmoil and strife to peace and
understanding, was but the consequence of a shift in my
personal perspective.

It delighted me, to be in charge, so naturally I thanked
them for it—everyone at the palace, the Cardinal, the various
chancellors, my mother, my younger brother, everyone.
I would have thanked even the servants, but my mother
stopped me, reminding me of the danger. (I was well-advised,
or so I believed, and thus was quick to accept all advice.)

Then one afternoon I had lunch with the Cardinal and my
mother, the first time since I was a boy that just the three of
us were able to be together. It was a nostalgic moment—tulip
poplars and dogwood blossoming outside the window, the
quiet clicks of servants crossing parquet floors to the table
with the chilled wines, the Dutch cheeses, the salted fish, the
crisp tan biscuits from England that I have loved since I was
a child. My mother's sweet, silvery vibrato mingled gracefully with the Cardinal's thin monotone and brought back a
rush of happy memories, images of slow, reassuring afternoons that I'd thought were gone forever.

The lunch had been my idea. I'd sent a note to the
Cardinal the previous morning, and to my mother that afternoon, saying, *I'd like the pleasure of your company for lunch*

tomorrow noon, in my chambers, signing with the name they
had given me years ago and had ceased using as soon as I'd
reached adolescence—*Zipper* (because of the scar, naturally).
My intention was to come right out and tell them both how
I was feeling about Things in General, a preview of my State
of the Kingdom Message, sort of. And then I had planned to
pick a date for the Coronation. With their respected advice
and consent, of course.

"More wine, Mother?"

She smiled her musical smile, nodded yes, and with the
lighter she wore around her neck on the gold chain Father
had given her, lit a cigarette and resumed her conversation
with my uncle the Cardinal.

"Excellency, more wine?"

He put two boney fingers to his lips, smiled thoughtfully,
and tapping the cross on his chest with the fingers of his other
hand, nodded yes, why not? I cannot remember him without
at least one hand tapping that cross. It's as if it were a tele-
graph key and he were constantly sending and receiving mes-
sages through it.

My mother was graciously quibbling with the Cardinal's
plan for my brother Paris' education. I couldn't blame her.
Ordinarily, I defer to Uncle Gordon's judgement in such
matters, but sending Paris to a large, midwestern university
was a ridiculous notion, based as it was on the popular view
of him as an extremely handsome athlete and party-goer.
Mother and I knew him better, though differently. We were
agreed, however, in believing him to own in nascent form a
personality that was essentially *gorgeous* (to be precise about
it). To our mind, therefore, one of the European capitals
seemed a more fitting place for such a fecund flower as Paris.
At Ohio State or the University of Illinois, he would be
brutalized.

"Mother?" I interrupted. "Excellency?"

"Yes, dear. What is it?" she asked.

"You're probably wondering why I've summoned you
here," I began.

There was a strange silence. I continued. "Well, as you
know . . . it's been over six months now, since the . . . ah,
well, since Father died. And, well, over two hundred days

now, two hundred fourteen, to be exact . . . since I . . . took
over, as it were. And . . . ah, well, I thought you'd like to
hear about how I see things . . . things in general, I mean. You
know."

"Why, yes, dear. Of course. That's a fine idea. Isn't it,
Gordon?"

The Cardinal peered at me over the rim of his glass. Returning the glass to the table, he said, "Indeed. How *do* you
see things? 'In general!' "

"Well . . . generally . . . I see it like a painting. A rough,
pastoral scene . . . like a Millet or an early Van Gogh. Calm.
Placid but not passive, exactly . . . busy, but contentedly so.
I *like* it. In fact, I've been trying to figure out exactly how
to tell you this, so you'd understand what I meant, exactly.
Because, I mean, well, it could get confused easily with something else. Like ambition . . . or greed, even. But to get right
down to it, what I want to say is that I'm happy. I like everything the way it is. The kingdom . . . well, you know how
I've always loved this place. The mountains, the plains from
sea to sea, the forests, the marshes and rivers, even the deserts!
The whole place! All of it. And the people, the good people
here, all the various classes and types, from the lowest peasant
all the way . . . to you two, sitting here before me! We're a
good people! We really are. And, well . . . now that I can see
things from all perspectives, I sort of see that everything is
working the way it's supposed to work, the industries, the
farms and trades, the transportation systems, the crafts and
various arts, the news media. It's like a perfectly tuned engine.
Therefore, I'm happy. And therefore, I would like to set a
date for the Coronation. I'm ready now to become the King,
for the rest of my life. . . ." I spread out my hands and
reached over to them, expecting them to clasp my hands in
their own.

But they let them hang there in the air, like half-filled
balloons. My mother looked puzzled, slightly, and turned to
the Cardinal, her brother, for an explanation. The Cardinal,
however, merely glared at me, as if I had uttered a name that
was contemptible to him.

"What's the matter?" I asked, incredulous.

"Let me understand. You are . . . happy?" the Cardinal
asked in a low voice.

"Ah . . . yes."

"And *therefore*, as a Crown Prince, you now wish to become King? I mean, officially, permanently?"

"Yes. But you must understand, this is not ambition."

"Oh?" The Cardinal had regained his composure. "Then, pray, what is it . . . if not raw, naked *ambition*?" He hurled the words at me with a disgust and violence I had not thought him capable of.

I was slightly angry now. After all, I did make myself painfully clear, and if they hadn't paid sufficient attention, it surely was not my fault. "Acceptance, Excellency. It's acceptance."

"*Acceptance*! Hah!" He sloshed more wine into his glass, drank it down in a gulp. "Acceptance. HAH!"

"Dear?" my mother said sweetly, politely, as if suddenly remembering a prior engagement. "I was wondering if you would like to have a masquerade party. You know, one of those grand masquerades, a three-day affair. How does that sound?"

"I don't know, okay, I guess. Fine." I honestly hadn't thought about that—a masquerade party. Could be fun.

"And we can use the occasion to announce the Coronation!" she exclaimed in a tinkling voice. "What a delightful idea!" Don't you think so, Gordon? To announce the Coronation at a masquerade party? To keep the whole thing a complete secret from everyone, except for the three of *us*, right up to the moment of unmasking, and *then* we'll announce it, the three of us together."

"Yes . . . a fine idea. Excellent. What about you, now, my sweet prince? Does that make you *happy*?" There was a touch of sarcasm in his voice that made me a little uncomfortable, but I decided to ignore it.

"Yes, wonderful idea. Thank you, Mother . . . and thank you, too, Excellency." I smiled openly. I believe, even now, that I was still saying things like that with total sincerity— that late in the development of the conspiracy. I was not a man easily made suspicious. My innocence clung like a leech.

Invitations, handsomely engraved, went out on schedule to everyone who mattered—the heads of the large corporations, the two union leaders, all the ministers of state and their

immediate families, those several admirals and generals who
participated in policy-making as a matter of course, a few
celebrities and famous athletes, a literary man, three or four
of the greater landowners in the kingdom, a half-dozen judges
and their wives, the more dignified members of the senate,
some provincial governors and their families, and the higher
clergy. About a month before the masquerade party was to
take place, the media-people started making their usual
noises, and by the time the event drew near, it had become,
for practically everyone in the kingdom, a national holiday.

Naturally, the plans for such a shindig were so complex
and far-reaching, yet so rooted in tradition and protocol, that
I shut the entire affair out of my mind and tried to go about
my daily business as if I had never even heard of the damned
thing. I confess, I was fast becoming annoyed with all the
fuss and gossip, the sloppy, wide-eyed anticipation filling the
eyes of secretaries, guards and servants. It was excessive. My
mother had become a tornado of social activity and planning,
whizzing through the corridors of the palace from morning
till after midnight. And whenever she happened to be still
and alone, she was inevitably talking urgently on the telephone—to florists, decorators, caterers, musicians, newspaper columnists. My uncle the Cardinal had left for Rome
again, promising my mother that he would be back with his
full entourage in plenty of time for the masquerade, bearing
gifts and political surprises, he added. But that was his usual
line when departing for the requisite stint at the Vatican,
anyhow. This time, however, my mother seemed to believe
him.

Exasperated, slightly confused by it all, I sought the company of my brother Paris. In recent years—except for the
month or so after our father the King had died—I'd spent
only occasional, brief, usually ceremonial moments with him,
which grieved me. As the first-born, I had early been separated
from Paris, and while my life had been fixed on the pole star
of leadership, the State, our father the King, etc., Paris had
been invited to fix onto the more diverting aspects of life in
a palace—food, exercise, sleep, young women and idle boys,
fast cars, beautiful clothing, etc. Evidently, we were both
obsessive types and thus we realized our respective roles

completely. But in spite of the awesome differences, whenever we met, however briefly or formally, great love passed between us, love and a profound pity, as if each of us were seeing in the other the mirrored image of his self's denial. I was completely what he was not, and he was the same for me. We completed each other. In some deep way, it was a terrifying kind of recognition, impossible to avoid.

"Hi, Zipper," he said as he entered the room. I had been reading Taine and hadn't heard him knock. He crossed the carpeted room to the bay window, where I stood with the book in my hand, and reaching delicately with his right hand, he touched the scar on my cheek with smooth, cool fingertips. I pressed the open palm of his hand to my lips and lightly kissed it. Our ancient greeting.

"Hello, Paris. Here, let me look at you," I gently ordered, standing away from him a second. He was gorgeously wrapped in deep blue silks, with a gold, gauze scarf casually wrapped around his head like a bandanna or headband, curly blond hair tumbling out at either side of it. Wearing soft, blue leather sandals, his supple, large, calf muscles exposed and rippling slightly as he moved, he looked like Hermes to me.

"You look so healthy, Paris!" I exclaimed, silently comparing his robust and graceful appearance to the way I felt. "Are you still able to work out as regularly as always?"

"Oh, who has the time?" he sighed and dropped himself onto a couch. "It's impossible now. I mean, impossible to spend the hours at it I used to. Before Father died, I mean. Now it's just one damned thing after another. You know. Boats to be launched, ribbons to be cut, roads to be opened, young cousins to be escorted about the town . . . the whole shitty she-bang. I can only imagine how it's been with you, Mister Crown Prince." He laughed affectionately. "And now there's this masquerade of Mother's! I mean, really. A masquerade! Whose drippy idea was that? Surely not yours?"

"No," I said. "It was her idea. It came up when I said I wanted to go ahead and have a Coronation."

"A *Coronation*!" Paris jumped up and gleefully whirled around the room. "Now that's an idea worth having! A Coronation! Who needs a fucky little masquerade when they can have an honest-to-god Coronation! You're a genius,

Zipper. But what happened? So how come we're going to
have a masquerade instead?" He dropped his lithe body
back onto the couch, curling his legs under him, and looked
at me eagerly.

"It's all supposed to be a secret. The bit about the Coronation, I mean. The idea is to announce the Coronation date
at the masquerade, when everyone takes off his mask." I
suddenly felt unnaturally weary. Maybe I didn't really want
to be king after all? Was it possible?

"Jee-*sus*! How boring."

"Yeah. Well, you're not supposed to know about the
Coronation Announcement part of it, so don't let on. Only
the three of us, I, Mother and Uncle Gordon, are supposed to
know. Okay?"

"No sweat. My lips are sealed. In fact, as a show of good
faith, *I'll* reveal a secret to *you*, one that only I, Mother and
dear old Uncle Excellency are supposed to know. But you'll
have to swear not to let them know I told you! I mean it."

"Sure."

"Okay. Guess who Mother will be dressed as when she
appears at the masquerade. Guess." Paris smiled snidely, a
trace of disgust creeping across his lips.

"I don't know . . . Peter Pan? Gloria Swanson? I don't
know. Tell me now, you know I hate guessing games." I
walked slowly back to the bay window.

"Me."

"What?"

"*Me*."

"Who?"

"*Me*. Paris, son of Oliver and Nahant. The Prince of
Dewey."

"Wow! How do you know that, for sure?"

"She told me. Well, she had to, I guess. I found out
about it from my friend Regis, the sculptor, who made some
rubber masks for her, not knowing the reason why she wanted
one of me. He just happened to mention it to me one evening,
very late and very drunk at a party thrown by Benedikt the
wine merchant's son. Regis, too, had been sworn to secrecy,
naturally, but he was *inexcuseably* drunk that night. Anyhow,
she had evidently gone to him because of his reputation for

making rubber likenesses of famous people for those environ-
mental sculptures of his, you know his work, quite popular,
and she'd asked him to make a full-face mask of me . . . and
also one of you, one of each of us, as life-like as possible. . . ."

"One of *me*?"

"Oh, yes, brother dear, you too. I confronted her on it.
I simply asked her what the hell she wanted with masks of
her beloved sons when the genuine articles were still so hale
and hearty, and she told me that she was planning to go to
the masquerade dressed as me, and our uncle His Excellency
Gordon Cardinal Nahant was to be dressed and masked as
you. Too much, eh?"

"Me? The Cardinal? Why?"

"Well . . . now that you've told me about the plans to
announce the Coronation and et cetera . . . well, maybe it
has something to do with that?" He smiled at me with false
timidity.

"May-be," I said, as understanding fell across me like a
velvet curtain.

"What are *you* planning to wear to the masquerade?"
Paris idly queried, intently staring at his fingernails.

"Honestly, I hadn't thought about it. Until now. But I
just this second had a marvelous idea. What about you?"

"Same idea," he said in a monotone, still studying his
manicure.

"Well, that settles it, then," I said, grinning with warmth
and heady anticipation. "How about a drink? Brandy?"

Paris accepted my offer readily, and he ended up staying
in my quarters the entire night, the two of us splitting two
bottles of fifty-year-old Napoleon brandy. Early the next
morning, with practically no hangovers—that's how fine the
brandy was—we went out looking for Paris' friend Regis, the
sculptor.

Everyone invited was there, of course. It was, as planned, a
grand affair, the costumes brilliantly inventive and mostly
erotic, the decorations tastefully lavish, the music exquisite,
refined, the food and conversation likewise . . . But, really,
there's no need to go into all that here, except simply to
note it as such. The truly important events, the only events

we are at all concerned with in the long run, were the un-
planned events—or, at least let me say, the *unannounced*
ones (God knows, they were rather on the well-planned side).

As predicted by her second son, Mother came dressed
and masked as her second son. Regis the sculptor did a decent
job of it, I have to admit, and even for those of us who happened to know Paris personally and well, it was at first difficult to know that the person we thought was he was not he
at all but rather was someone masquerading as him the way
he used to be.

There was a long-limbed, boney, young man dressed as a
purple and blue harlequin standing near the entrance portals
on the ballroom side of the velvet arras, and when Mother-as-
Paris entered, he had nodded in her direction and had said
tunefully, "Oh that Paris! What a *metaphysical* costume, to
come dressed as himself! Who else would have *thought* of it,
I ask you!" That's how the more perceptive individuals in
the group perceived it.

Of course, this was before I—or rather, the Cardinal—had
made an entrance. When he did come into the ballroom, he
entered from behind the arras to my left and therefore
slightly behind me as well, for I had preceded him from that
hallway into the ballroom by not more than a pair of steps,
coming along as I did behind Paris, who'd managed cleverly
to time his arrival for a few critical seconds behind Mother.
That boy knew what he was doing, right from the start. I
was smart to trust him.

To anyone already in attendance at the ball, to the
young bruise-colored harlequin, say, things probably would've
appeared this way: first Mother would have swept into the
room, down the half-dozen carpeted stairs at the central
entryway, and he would at that point have exclaimed, "Oh
that Paris! What a *metaphysical* costume . . . ," etc.

In a moment, however, Mother's mannish gait and somewhat . . . machismo manner—her understandably flawed
imitation of her son's gait and manner—would have betrayed
her to the harlequin and to anyone else who'd ever admired
Paris' characteristic gait and manner. Respect and honor
would have been swiftly withdrawn, to be replaced with disgust slightly mixed with envy: "What a ballsy idea for a

costume, dressing up as the Prince of Dewey, but who would be so *gauche*?"

And then came Paris himself, dressed as Mother, but in his case, it's a perfect imitation, crown jewels and all, sable, ermine and fox, royal blue velvet with hammered gold trim, white taffeta ruffles and cuffs, a short, diamond-encrusted baton held delicately in his right hand, silvery-blond hair stuffed with pearls and piled atop his head like a ziggurat. He was gorgeous. Nodding to his left and right, accepting homage, compliments, dismay, confusion and love with benign pleasure, he swept into the room, lightly touched fingertips with Mother (his second son) as he passed, forcing her to acknowledge and honor his queenly presence, crossed the huge, cavernous ballroom to the opposite side, mounted the dais there, and took his seat upon the Queen's throne. Then he smiled regally upon the awe-struck multitude and waited for me to enter.

Upon Paris' entering the ballroom, however, the crowd had parted like the Red Sea for the Jews and had left a wide alley from the doorway across the floor to the dais, and it was into this wholly unexpected gauntlet of space that the Cardinal stumbled, unfortunately dressed and masked as the Crown Prince. Astonished, he saw the Queen seated in her proper place, upon the throne next to that of the King, as on all sides came short bursts of applause from the assembly, some rough huzzahs and cries, first, of, "Long live the Crown Prince!" and then, "Let's hear it for the Zipper!" The Cardinal grabbed his cheek, the cheek of his mask, remembering suddenly that scar which had been placed upon my cheek so long ago in play by my brother, and naturally he felt no such scar on his own cheek (Regis would not be so crudely realistic as to include scars and other unsightly facial marks on our masks). Amid the cries and cheers of the crowd, then, glaring darkly at the Queen, whom he wrongly supposed to be my mother, for having betrayed him at the last minute, he stumbled over his feet (unaccustomed as he was to the wearing of heavy, cowskin boots) and fell down, losing all remaining composure and temper simultaneously, stamping his heels against the floor in a tantrum as he lay there. Then, leaping to his feet, he ran back out the door to the hallway, and glimpsing me standing there as he rushed past, his face was suddenly flooded with shock and fear, and he stopped short in his flight and fell to his knees, begging with a weepy, broken voice, "Your majesty, your beneficient, all-forgiving majesty, *please!*"

I peered down at him, acknowledging his presence, and informed him that I would deal with him later and that for now I expected him to change his "costume" and present himself as quickly as possible in his usual clerical garb. I told him where he could find me, and then, wearing the crown comfortably and with only the most casual restraint of my movements, I proceded into the ballroom, nodding and smiling easily to the shouts and rising cries of the people as I walked across the smooth floors to the dais and mounted the steps to the throne next to the Queen and took my proper seat. With a wave of my hand, I ordered the dancing to begin, and immediately it began.

IMPASSE

He stood near a curtained French door leading out of
the livingroom to another room off it. He was slouching, as
if about to reach out and touch the door, to open it. But
turning slowly away, he crossed the room to the far corner
opposite and sat down in an overstuffed, maroon armchair.
Rain sloshed against the window next to him. Without
getting up, he snapped on the floor lamp. Lit a cigarette.
Stood again. Crossed the uncarpeted floor of the large room
and went into a tiny, windowless alcove that apparently
functioned as a kitchen. Grabbing a bottle of beer from the
refrigerator, he opened it and returned to the livingroom, sat
down in the chair again and took a long pull from the bottle.
He listened to the beer in his mouth and throat, and to
the rain, the footsteps overhead, a muffled radio somewhere down the hall, to the cars on the street below hurridly
splashing past the building, a bus sloshing to a stop at the
corner. He got up again and went to the window, pulled
back the heavy, red velvet drape with one hand and looked
intently out.
The rush hour traffic was building, sliding rapidly along
the streets, accumulating suddenly at intersections. Across
the street, in haze, spread the Fens, a large, yellowish-green
park with bogs, old Back Bay canals, flowergardens, some
grass, ball fields and occasional trees. And beyond the Fens,
along its western edge, the four- and five-storey, blond brick
apartment houses, houses built over a half-century ago for
the parents and grandparents of the young people living in
them now. The blackened windows of the apartments, one
by one, turned yellow. He imagined wives flicking on kitchen
lights and beginning to prepare suppers for small families,

husbands coming wetly in from the halls to read their newspapers in slowly dimming livingrooms.

He could see the windows of his own apartment. They
stared blackly onto the park from just above the tops of
a clutch of four or five elm trees. There was a crowded
boulevard between the trees at the edge of the park and
the building itself, but he couldn't see that boulevard at all,
not even the moving tops of the cars, from where he was
standing. What was she doing now? he wondered. Why
weren't the lights on yet? The windows—flat against the
wall, rectangular, cold—stubbornly refused to come suddenly
to life with the warm light from inside the kitchen, while he
stared helplessly across the park, waiting.

"You can see your apartment pretty nicely from there,
can't you?" she said. He turned around slowly. Rosa had
come out of the bedroom, was closing the French doors behind her, her long hands hidden behind her. Somehow, he had
assumed that she would re-emerge from the bedroom dressed
in a gown that flowed seductively along at her feet, with her
hair freshly loosened, combed out and falling across her bare
shoulders. But she was still wearing a khaki workshirt and
levis cut off above the knee, and her hair was wound around
her head like a shopkeeper's wife. She wore no makeup, as
before, and seemed totally uninvolved with the facts of his
presence, as before.

Flopping her long body into the chair he had just vacated,
she lit a mentholated cigarette and again observed that one
could see Ham's apartment pretty nicely from her window,
couldn't one?

He mumbled, yes, one could, and resumed watching the
tiny black squares across the park. Still nothing, he thought.
Where is she? Busy, doing errands? Out buying food for the
meal he would miss? Was she out on the street somewhere, in
the rain, with the baby? he wondered, suddenly horrified by
the possibility that she would come here, looking for him,
pathetically asking Rosa: "Have you seen Ham. He isn't home
yet and when I called the bookstore the man there said that
he left at noon feeling sick."

"I ought to go home," he said, turning around to face
Rosa, who sat, one leg thrown across the arm of the chair,

watching her cigarette smoke drift in blue spirals to the
high, beamed ceiling.

"In this rain? You'll be drenched."

He agreed, took his half-emptied bottle of beer from the
windowledge and crossed the room to the piano and sat down
heavily on the bench. He thought: She's got to be well-off to
afford this place, to know enough to furnish it sparsely, to
hang only original paintings on the walls even though it means
she hang but three or four. But she wasn't even a *working*
musician, he remembered. She was a student.

He decided that someone must be keeping her, someone
who pays for all this. Some married man, probably, five or so
years older than she, ten or so years older than he. Some nice
guy with a good job in an advertising firm on Arlington Street,
or maybe a TV executive, who lived with a wife and three
kids in a big, new house in the suburbs. A guy trying to make
his life interesting by keeping a bohemian mistress and spend-
ing one weekend a month with her to get his money's worth,
the kind of man whose father would have done the same
thing at the same age and told him about it when the son
turned twenty-one.

That would explain everything, Ham thought. Her
apparent solitude, her comfortable living conditions, her
strange indifference to his presence. Not indifference, actually:
simply her willingness to treat him as a casual friend, a
neighbor, when in fact it was perfectly clear that his interest
in her was sexual, had been from the very first time he saw
her, at a party, four weeks ago. Asking who she was, he had
been told, by a girl who studied at the Conservatory with
her and claimed to know her well, that Rosa had once been
the mistress of a now-famous jazz musician. From that night
on, he had tried to place himself so that he and Rosa could
be at the same place at the same time, which wasn't difficult,
as it turned out, since several of his friends quickly revealed
that they were friends of Rosa as well. So he simply spent
all his free time with those particular people, ignoring his
usual comrades, who knew Rosa only casually, if at all.

He had let it be known to her right away that he was
married—mentioning Charleen's name to her casually in a
restaurant, the restaurant where he had placed himself at

noon one day, calculatedly near the door, after having seen
her go there for lunch the day before. The bookstore where
he worked was located four doors down from the small,
cafeteria-style restaurant, and the Conservatory was across
the avenue from both, right next to the Northeastern University classroom buildings. The place was usually jammed by
12:05 with students, and unless one shared a table with
friends or acquaintances, one usually ended up standing near
the door, waiting fifteen or twenty minutes for an empty
table to appear.

He had already finished eating and was drinking his
second cup of coffee when she came in, alone. She looked
swiftly across the crowded room in search of a free table,
saw none, then saw him, and smiled. He waved her over, told
her to share his table with him, he was leaving in a minute
anyway. He stayed, and they talked, and he mentioned
Charleen's name.

The same thing happened the next day, and the next,
and then it had become a part of their daily routines—to
have lunch together. He held onto the saving grace of
necessity, however. Simply, he was able to leave the
store early enough to secure a table in the crowded restaurant, which a few minutes later she was able to share with
him.

They had become "friends", even to the point of her
inviting him to drop by her apartment, for coffee, anytime
he happened to be in the neighborhood. He had explained
that they were neighbors, that he was in her neighborhood
often, and thus he might be dropping by for coffee any day
now, if her invitation still held. She had assured him that it
did, and he had gone back to the store thinking that if he
were to be placed in a situation with her whereby he would
have to say Yes or No, he would not be able to say No and
would end up sleeping with her, no matter what the consequences—and he could not conceive of there being no
consequences: with his sleeping with Rosa and Charleen
not finding out about it. But he could not believe that having
done it once he would not do it again and again, until either
Rosa had fallen in love with him, or he with her, or both.
And any one of those three possibilities, even without Charleen's knowing, would be consequential.

But if Charleen did find out, she would be unable to do anything less than leave him, he thought. All her terrors would have been justified, and the only person capable of convincing her otherwise would be Ham, and then only after years, years of shame-faced atonement and reassurances, which he knew he could never bring himself to offer. Not anymore. Not now. To reassure her constantly that he loved her and would never leave her, even while remaining faithful to her, was painfully difficult. But to do the same thing, after having slept with another woman, would be for him physiologically impossible.

He did not love Charleen, he told himself. He never had, and thus, without ever loathing or even disliking her, he loathed himself for being married to her. It wasn't her fault. It was his. She hadn't lied. He had. And though he wanted desperately to be able, somehow, to blame her for it, even for a part of it, he couldn't, and so he wouldn't. Leaving her now, telling her the truth and walking out, seemed to him as loathesome as its opposite act, marrying her in the first place. All acts that seemed to him necessarily moral had been neutralized by an opposing set of necessarily moral acts, and as a result, he hung motionless between two polarized alternatives, unable to accept or reject either one.

He had swung back and forth from one alternative to the other, day after day, until finally, repelled by his own inability to choose one of two kinds of guilt, he had left the store at noon, did not meet Rosa for their usual lunch, and instead, walked all the way down Massachusetts Avenue to the Charles River, and then had strolled slowly along the grassy bank of the river for an hour or so, watching the Harvard and M.I.T. sculls cutting slickly through the choppy, grey water and the pinwheeling clusters of seagulls and terns moving gradually inland along the river from the Bay, and when it had begun to rain, he had scrambled up the bank to the street. He had found himself standing on Commonwealth Avenue, less than a block from Kenmore Square and only two blocks from Rosa's apartment, about ten blocks from his own.

The rain had come all at once and heavily. He ran down Commonwealth Avenue, across Kenmore Square, and then around the corner onto Beacon Street. He stepped up to

the doorway, found her name over one of the mailboxes and
pushed the small, white button next to her name. When she
had asked who was it from the tiny, square speaker near the
ceiling, he had called back his own name in a voice he did
not recognize.

She laughed, a tinny, electric voice from the speaker
overhead. "Are you soaked?" she asked.

"Not really!" he called. "But I will be if you don't push
the button that opens this door, so I can come up and wait
out the rain before going on home."

"Fine," she said, and pressed the button that opened the
door to the inside lobby.

He had thought that the rain wouldn't last, that it was a
summer shower and would move quickly inland and break
up against the hills in a half-hour or so. But it rained all
afternoon, while they talked and drank beer, talking first of
music and musicians—in which she was the teacher and he
the rapt student—and then of people, friends, and finally of
his marriage—in which he was the speaker and she the listener,
the poser of questions.

He told her mainly of his dilemma, little else. As it turned
out, Rosa seemed interested in little else, seemed almost eager
to have him continue speaking of his marriage in the abstract,
problematic terms he so adored. She agreed, at last, that he
had reached an impasse, there was no doubt. And then, as if,
having found the right word, "impasse", she were no longer
concerned with its context or the situation to which it
applied, she'd gotten up from her chair, saying that she'd
be right back, and had gone into the bedroom.

Now she was back in the livingroom again, sitting across
from him in her maroon armchair, looking bored and slightly
impatient—while he sat on the piano bench and tried to decide whether or not she was being kept by someone, whether
or not he ought to leave now, whether or not Charleen was
out looking for him, since it was after six and he knew she
would have called the store long ago, and whether or not he
should, could, take the chances that he knew he would take.

It was Rosa who decided, not me, he could conclude,
afterwards, if he ever found himself once again going back

to that rainy night, questioning it, re-enacting it, step by step and word by word, until at last he could feel that he had it right, all of it, even to the smell of her hair and the exact intonations of her voice, the precise fall of the light in the room, as she came across to him and sat down facing him and placed her long, thin hands on his hips, telling him that he should feel free of anything that so clearly had come to be an impasse, that there was no other way to break the balance between two alternatives than to create a third alternative. And smiling, as if happy for him now. And then tightening against him as he kissed her, moving her arms around him. And whispering against his pressing face that it's fine, it's fine, it's all right, don't worry, she would let him lead her from the bright, high-ceiling'd, hall-like living-room to the close darkness and warmth of the bedroom. There, in total silence, he would make love to her, shoving himself again and again against her quick, twisting body, bringing her rapidly through to the other side of her intent with relentless, soundless thrusts. Then driving himself through, too, his body blossoming out from its still center, spreading, turning from tree to flower, to cloud, to motion-less, shapeless pool of water in darkness and silence. And oh, the clarity that would follow.

THE DRIVE HOME

. . . So far as I can see now, there are but two directions
available to me, just two, and no more. In and Out. All
others, which most people claim are different, new directions,
simply are not. They must be either In or Out.

If she thinks to ask me:

Up or Down?
North or South?
East or West?
North by Northwest or South by Southeast?
That or This?
From or To?

I will have to answer, No. These, as well as any others
already mentioned inadvertently in passing, all these sets of
directions are best understood as In or Out. Whether in or
out of context.

I simply can't see it any other way. Not even circular
(an absurd notion, relevant perhaps to the experiences of
plants and some lower animals, but thankfully no longer
regarded by *any*one in *any* field as even remotely relevant
to human experience—which disregard, admittedly, imposes
a bit of a come-down on us human animals, regardless of
the pride we take in the efficiency with which truth is being
served).

No. Not even circular.

I don't want to digress, but it's strange, how every time,
when I seem to begin, I have the distinct impression that I
am absolutely alone, as if standing in the middle of an
enormous room, whose walls are too far away for me to
see in this gloomy light. And then in a very short time I
discover that all along what I thought I was presenting to

myself alone was actually being uttered to someone else. And then I realize that either I am not alone or else I am what is usually called "mad". *Viz.*, I speak: therefore I'm heard. Yet *that* makes absolutely no sense whatsoever, even to me, and surely not to anyone who happens to be listening out for something worth listening to.

But to return. In and/or Out. The move In and/or the move Out.

The first is nearly completed now; the second will begin soon. An arrival, as such, should not be looked for, any more than a point of departure should. They have been ignored here, as everywhere. . . .

This is so damned *difficult*! It's not even circular. I sometimes try to console myself and family by saying that if we weren't alive, we wouldn't even be interested in life. Some consolation.

(Surely the dreams that afflict other people's lives are not so fucking ultimate! What I wouldn't give for a little symbolism now and then. Or myth, even.)

(All my dreams and, therefore, all my acts as well, seem to end parenthetically, even when busted apart by the alarm clock. The alarm clock! Now *there's* a symbol for you!

. . . A willing girl spreads like a coffee-colored flower with a still-darker center, and I grow heavy with infamy by mid-afternoon.

Driving home in sleet to wife and tiny daughter. Windshield wipers shuffling the scene before me with each swipe of the blade.

Boston.

The industrial suburbs.

The residential suburbs.

Moving out from the tight, black center, like a pale insect—sated, bloated, staggering heavily away. . . .

Driving. Bent over my work intently, one hand on the inside of either thigh, thumbs working the brown flesh, working it up, palms and fingers pressing thighs down; brown, round ass down flat against the mattress; holding her down; down; down. . . .

Outside, icy rain noisily slops into the streets, falls

across these high, narrow, brick buildings, sloshes along
gutters, choking the sewers.

I tell her none of this, I tell her nothing, except what
she expects and desires to hear from me, here, doing this
infamous thing to her. Later, I tell her what I was thinking
at the time—because she asks. (You want to know what I
was thinking while I was fucking her? All right, if that
somehow gratifies you, I'll tell you. I wonder what you'll
make of it.) This:

I was worrying about how I could not forget where I
was and what I was doing. No, really. *Worrying* about it.
Who can forget where they are and what they are doing,
when they are fucking in these cities, these cold, blackened
crematoriums, where all the people crowd up against the
fences, pushing and shoving weakly for a chance to stare
out at the ones who years ago, when there must have been
more room for fewer people, got away. They smile back from
outside, looking somehow quaint, the men reading their
newspapers, the women dressed in white starched aprons,
beating tan batter in wooden bowls. Even . . . no, *especially*
my wife and daughter, seen from here, seem no longer to
have anything to do with me. I recognize them as distant,
dead relatives seen in a daguerreotype. My daughter chirps
like a bird in a warm kitchen. My wife prepares an evening
meal, smiling as she works. They have no names.

I am all name, and as a result am heavy with infamy. . . .

You crazy, she says, thinking something else (but not
the *fact* of thinking something else).

I'm not insane. No sir. Nor ashamed. I'm guilty, that's
what. Shame can be but for a single act, guilt is for all
existence. The price and the consequence.

There ain't no way around it, I tell her. One simply
must go for the center, the dark hole that opens for him, and
with hands, feet and mouth wide open and reaching, to touch
everything—wet ceilings, flaking walls, scaly floors cold
against bare feet. And lifting suddenly, he will come to life,
like a huge motor starting up. The past turns into a picture-
magazine that he flipped through once while waiting for
someone to come into the room and call his name (The
Doctor will see you now, Mr. Bass.) and tell him what he's

dying of. Of being a father. A husband. A Causasian. A Ph.D. A twenty-five year old American male. A high school teacher of American history. Of being the owner of a 1959 Chevrolet Impala sedan. Of being a registered Democrat in the town of Wakefield, Massachusetts. Of being the husband of a nineteen-year-old blonde from Hartford, Connecticut. Of being the only child of parents dying silently, slowly, in Crawford, New Hampshire. Of being the friend of a friend, with no friends of his own. Of being an insomniac who dreams. An adulterer. A wife-beater. A cheater at cards. Tall man. Heavy man. Of being a quiet man. A formal man. A cold man. Stingy man. Of being a ridiculous man . . . a woefully ridiculous man, full of pity for himself. *These* kinds of things, presumably, one needs to hear from others. This is why they must keep on talking to us. For we are taught to believe, by each other, that we cannot exist without first coming to know, and constantly coming to know again, these kinds of things about ourselves. And then, as a consequence, we die— as if to prove the truth of what we've just been told. . . .

The truth is subtler stuff, though. And less easily complied with. For the truth is that I cannot need to know these kinds of things, if I also need to exist. They are important to me only if I'm in a hurry to die. They are the things for which I must feel only passing pride or redeemable shame.

No. Guilt is the meaningful consequence, the one meaningful consequence . . . the one desirable consequence.

Give it to me, baby! she cries to the ceiling.

Take it! I reply. Take it, take it!

Give it to me, baby! Don't hurt me!

Take it, take it, take it!

Give it to me! Oh Jesus, Jesus!

Take it . . . take it . . . take it . . . !

And then I come, deep inside her, all at once and from every direction, like a full jug, shattering. . . .

She pounds me on the head with her fists, beats at my ears and eyes, cheeks, nose and lips, moaning. . . .

While dressing, I peer through the soot-covered window and watch the people down below on the street. Cringing in grey light beneath the cold rain. Hiding under newspapers, hats, umbrellas. Scurrying along sidewalks in dark, heavy clothing.

You good, baby. You make it, honey, you really make it.
More of the same, I tell her. That's all there is.

. . . And I have dreams of being caught, as by a photograph,
in certain postures and with facial expressions, representing
me at the precise instant of the climax of some athletic
event. (Here I am exhibiting my now-famous high-Yankee
bellyroll, as I go up and over the high-jump bar. As if I am
actually floating in the air! Notice, in the background, the
curious mixture of disappointment, chagrin and sheer disbelief beginning to spread across the Russian jumper's
face. . . .)

But I also have dreams of spinning suddenly on my heels,
raising a high-powered rifle to my shoulder, aiming cooly
down the barrel at a creature moving rapidly along the
rocky bank of a mountain stream, and—when I have let
the tip of the barrel hover cruelly above the creature's
head for barely a second—dropping it to the head, squeez-
ing the trigger. As if one move necessitated the other! (Here
the dream ends, for it is not of my killing the creature, but
of my firing the gun . . . Then it repeats.)

These two types of dreams in recent years have literally
plagued my sleep and now have become as images for me.
Images to me, actually. And for my "identity". Insofar
as my identity can be said to concern me. To and/or for
me.

This is because I am a thief and a murderer. Like all
thieves and murderers, I am many other things as well, but
it is only as a thief and murderer that I concern myself with
myself. For while we are asleep here, we are awake elsewhere, and thus every man is at least two men.

Images, however, have no psychological or psycho/
sociological significance for me. None whatsoever. I feel
able to affirm this, to employ it as a basic premise in any
examination of my self, because I have no doubt but that
I am located at the very center of the universe and am,
thereby, its prime mover. Such an attitude toward the universe and its center and the necessary relation between the
two (i.e., one of them being necessarily the mover of the
other, and thus the "prime" mover) may well be little more
than an unconscious response to the all-pervasive notion of a

heliocentric solar system; but even if this *is* so, I cannot help it, nor can I ever know it for sure, and so I do not intend to try (helping or knowing).

Therefore, when I am asked, Why, Fletcher, do you steal? I am able to answer freely, Because I am a thief. And to, Why do you murder? I reply: Because I am a murderer.

The nub of me, then, must be metaphysical. *E.g., belief.*

And the nature of my enterprise—to uncover the nub—casts me in the role of metaphysician. Given these premises, I am perhaps the diagnostician of my own soul, but only if the diagnosis give up evidence that a prognosis will be required. Otherwise, my enterprise will have been purely analytical, which, while not a *totally* fruitless activity, still doesn't give quite the ethical dignity of the other.

The most recent—and in many ways the most clear-cut—evidence that I am a thief and a murderer turned up this morning, shortly before dawn. This must be regarded as incontrovertible proof. Then I will move on to a much more tangled matter, *i.e.*, the question of meaning. That is, the "So what" of the question.

But to cite the evidence:

This morning, before it began fading into light, I stole a small glass of Irish whiskey from a bottle that had been left out on a liquor cabinet the night before, and I killed a little girl, who was about ten years old, I would guess, and who had gotten up before anyone else in the house. Passing the door to the living room while on her merry way to the bathroom, she discovered me there and demanded to know what I was doing, drinking her Daddy's whiskey. I hit her on the head with a poker and left the house by the cellar door, the same way I had entered the house hours before. As always, I was confused, but not, as in the past, mortified. (Mortification is essentially the result of having been surprised. Once such things were no longer capable of surprising me, they were unable to mortify me. This, in spite of my continuing to become horribly confused.)

Well and good, but "So what?" one might say.

Indeed. So this:

So now I endure dreams of standing before a liquor cabinet in an unfamiliar, shadow-banked living room, a half-

filled glass of excellent Irish whiskey in my hand. Old
Bushmill's

A little girl, probably about ten years old and dressed
in her flannel nightgown, pads barefoot down the hall, passes
the living room, and accidentally, casually, peers into the
gloom of the room and sees me.

What are you doing, drinking my Daddy's whiskey? His
very favorite too, she adds. Amazingly unruffled for a child
her age.

I put the glass down, grab a poker from beside the fireplace, and before the tyke has had a chance to realize what
I am up to, I have killed her, felled her with a single blow,
have wiped all fingerprints from all touched objects and am
disappearing silently down the cellar steps, a genie returning
to his lamp. . . .

Images, then, multiply uncontrollably, and with incredible speed. And so must the things they represent. Or I would
have wakened and been punished long ago.

. . . It's not unusual for me to while away an evening at
home by sitting in my green chair listening to Verdi. *Falstaff*, his swan-song, is my favorite. Thus it is even less unusual if I happen to be tapping my foot to *Falstaff* (Act
II).

The Boston *Globe*, refolded along its original creases,
lying beside the chair like a good dog, headlines pressed
to the floor. The apartment silent, except for the music. The
roars of Falstaff's courting, emitted from a machine squatting
across the room from me, seeming to emphasize the silence
of the five other rooms in the flat. Maroon, cracked-leather
slippers on feet. Necktie loosened. Cardigan unbuttoned.
Eyeglasses on the table next to the chair, thumb and forefinger of right hand rubbing dents on either side of bridge of
nose. Gray odor of boiled cabbage still hanging in the air,
sneaking up nostrils, spreading corrosively through con-
volted passageways up behind eyes and forehead. . . .

None of this is unusual for me.

My hero need not despair of continuing this dreary
normalcy, however. He is a cocksman now. And in a
second or two, he will rise from his green, thick-limbed

chair's hug, will turn up the volume of his portable record player, and will tramp authoritatively down the dim hall to the bathroom at the end. For he is a cocksman now, and a cocksman, as Archilochos says, must keep his prick clean and dainty.

Mistress Quickly's voice in the background, Falstaff's barreling from the huge wicker hamper next to the wall, Mr. Ford's raging on either side of Mistress Quickly's . . . I flop my prick over the cold, white edge of the sink, watch it shrink back and feel my balls (still inside my pants) drawing up from the shock of the cold. Rather small for a cocksman's.

Not so much small, actually, as tempermental. Enormous, scarlet, quivering like a fresh-caught Spanish mackerel when enticed. Tiny, brown, and flaccid when challenged or ignored. And having rid myself of wife and child, I am prepared to have it enticed. I slosh it around in warm water for a few moments, dry it carefully with a face towel and place it back into my pants, dropping it and feeling its nice weight down there in the warmth and darkness of my crotch.

Checking (coat and muffler on): record-player off, no gas jets left on in the kitchen, all but the hall light turned off, wallet in pocket, money in wallet, cigarettes, matches, comb in shirt pocket. He closes the door, steps into the gloom of the stairwell landing, turns back to the door and locks it. Drops the keys back into his coat pocket. Sniffs: the cooking smells of five kitchens—two on the first floor, two on the second, and one on his, the third—sweep through his head like a swarm of houseflies. Descending two flights of stairs to the street will be unpleasant for him.

Checking again: gloves in coat pocket, one in each, keys in right pocket, car key on ring.

Then I remember: Oh, the *car*! She took the car with her!

You take the car and I'll have you arrested for stealing it! I had screeched into her face. I mean it! We're not just a-playing around now, lady! No sir! You take that car and I'll have a warrent for your arrest sworn out in five minutes!

You've been watching too much television, she muttered, going back to the task of buttoning Linda's coat. Linda sat on the chair, unable to move in her clothes and looking,

inside coat, leggings, hat, scarf, mittens and fur-lined boots,
like an overstuffed teddy bear being pushed, prodded and
pulled about by an angry teenager. That's no teenager, that's
my wife. What're you going to do, Dagmar? I calmly asked,
leaning back against the kitchen sink, folding my arms com-
placently across my chest. Run home to Mama and Papa,
taking *them* your child, like a teenager again? Is that what
you want? Is that what I'm keeping you from? Huh? C'mon,
let's hear it! I'm keeping you from being a teenager! That's
really it, isn't it! I smiled—as if I had just explained some
self-evident truth to my students. American History 101-A.
The "bright" students. Hah! I'll show 'em who's bright.
Compared to them, to her, I'm a goddam Christmas tree.

You know, I observed, lighting a cigarette and blowing
blue jets of smoke out my nostrils, you know, Dagmar, you
really aren't too different from the little teenage tarts I see
sitting out there in front of me every day. Cud-chewing,
empty-headed, purple-sweatered cunts. That's *all* they are,
you know. The correspondances are self-evident, m'dear.

She stood up, slowly, stiffly. Linda, at last, was capable
of facing the elements. Will you *please* shut up? she said to
me, lifting the child off the chair and placing her onto the
floor in a standing position. Then she went to the coat closet,
took her long, gray, tweed coat from a wire hanger and
climbed into it.

And the same goes for Linda too! I yelled to her, with
Linda, having heard her name, struggling vainly to turn
around and face her accuser. I mean, the same as goes for
the car! You take this child out of here and I'll swear out a
warrent for your arrest on kidnapping charges! Then I'll get
a divorce on grounds of desertion, which'll give *me* custody
of the child!

You can't win, I smiled, as she returned to the kitchen.

Fletcher, she said in a low voice. Fletch, please. You've
got to stop this now . . . please. You've taken just about
everything I have . . . *including* my love for you. Please know
that. Please know that I don't love you anymore. I don't
even care what comes out of your mouth anymore. So
please know what is happening now . . . to you . . . to me,
and for God's sake, know what is happening to Linda! The

marriage is over, Fletcher . . . You've killed it. *Please* recognize the plain fact of its *death*! Don't you know that we can't fight anymore? Fighting with each other is something people can do only when there's still some kind of life left in their marriage . . . and ours is dead. It doesn't even matter who killed it. . . .

You're perfectly right, I told her. Which is why I'm so concerned about Linda and the car. When there's nothing else, one turns to protecting his property. And as for Linda, my concern is simply that you don't take her out in the streets at this late hour with no definite place to go. Your parents live several hundred miles from here, as you know, and you have no money to get there by public transportation. Your friends . . . well, if you *have* any friends who will put you up, *I* don't know them.

She sighed. She was very tired by then.

Fletcher, give me the key to the car. I have a credit card for gas and I'll only use it to buy enough gas to get to Hartford . . .

See! You *are* running home to Mama and Papa!

Just until I can figure out what to do after that. Now give me the key. Please.

Sorry, Dagmar. I refuse to aid you in this . . . this escapade, in any way whatsoever. Nor will I force you to *stay*, of course. As far as I am concerned, you are an adult. Regardless of your desires to be treated like a teenager.

Fletcher . . . please.

Linda began to cry. I looked at her.

I think that you have gone insane, she announced quietly. I don't know what else to think . . . because if you haven't gone insane, then everything else has been insane all along . . . right from the beginning. Never mind about the car key. I think I have my own in the glove compartment. (The first time I knew about *that*.) Then she picked Linda up in her arms and walked out of the kitchen, down the hall, and out the door. I listened to her clump, clump, clump, down the stairs, her heavy steps growing fainter and fainter as she descended, until finally I couldn't hear them anymore.

It was so quick . . . and so easy.

I walked out onto the landing. Heard the building door

CARL A. RUDISILL LIBRARY
LENOIR RHYNE COLLEGE

hissing as it closed on the street, and a few seconds later, the
easily recognizable, clear, sweet rumble of the Corvette
coming to life where I had parked it out in front of the building this afternoon. The blood rushed into my head and then
as quickly drained, and I felt suddenly chilled, standing out
there on the landing.

He locks the door slowly behind him, walks down the
hall to the coat closet, sheds his coat and goes into the living
room. Loosening his tie and unbuttoning his cardigan, kicking
off loafers and sliding his feet into old slippers, he sets Verdi's
Falstaff on the record player, flicks the machine on and
drops his body into his green armchair. This is the way he
usually spends his evenings. Toward the end of the second
act, he falls asleep. Sitting up. In the chair. Thumb and
forefinger of his right hand pressing. Either side of the
bridge. Of his nose.

. . . There is an order to this. There is a continuum. Though
they are not the same here, no more than anywhere else.
But nevertheless, there is no beginning, nor is there an ending.
I can't say otherwise, for I can express things no more
honestly than I can experience them. If I go backwards,
then, or cross over, it is only towards what I mean—as
someone once said, someplace. And while there may well
be uncovered a progression here, there is no progress as
such. . . .

The young lady next to me on the bus keeps smiling
primly straight ahead, across her boney knees and out the
huge wall-like windshield, to the road that seems to be
laying itself down before us, a black ribbon between mounds
and fields of snow on either side. The girl's light blue ski
sweater is covered with fine, white angel-hair, making her
look hazy from neck to waist. Her face is a young Christian's:
confident, complaisant, and pitying, all at once, and consequently, she looks at me with gratitude and pity, when she
can no longer stare straight ahead and be polite about it.

Bored, I give up trying to impress her stolid taste with
intellectual filigree and go back to looking out the window
on my other side.

Across the aisle from the girl sits a big, blond, crew-cut

boy of twenty or so, no larger than I but in much better
shape, and he knows her needs instinctively, whereas I would
have difficulty even learning them by rote. His is the suggestion that we sing. We—the skiers and I. His, too, the
guitar. And the songs.

Which they all sing with gusto. They—the skiers. Two
or three songs they must have learned from Pete Seeger
records owned by their roommates at college. I nod my
head in time to the music, smiling gently—to show her the
range of my tolerance, I suppose.

Then the blond guy across the aisle from her, seeing
that not quite all of the skiers on the bus appreciate his
enthusiasm (since it *is* still rather early in the day), suggests
loudly that whoever wants to have a "sing-along" (his expression) should join him and his trusty guitar at the rear
of the bus, where there happen to be many vacant seats. He
stands up in the middle of the aisle, guitar in hand, and
coaxes the Christian lady to follow him to the rear of the
bus, where, we all know, it will be darker, more intimate,
and further from the father-figure in the military uniform,
the fat man driving the bus implacably northward, than
where we are now seated—in the front row, with only the
driver and the exit steps between us and the great wall of
glass.

Hey, c'mon, whyn't we all go sing in the back! C'mon,
everybody, there's loads of room back there and we won't
have to bug the driver that way! C'mon! Everybody who
wants to sing, move to de back ob de bus! (Suburban white
wit, I smile tolerantly to my Christian lady, who missed
it and thus cannot comprehend my response, its dignity.)
C'mom, he says to my lady. Say, what's your name, anyhow? Mine's Buzz, he says proudly.

Mine's Fletcher, I murmur into her tiny ear. Fletcher
Bass.

Mine's Cynthia, she tells Buzz. Cynthia, she repeats to
me compassionately, lifting her hard, broad, and nearly
shapeless, wool-skirted ass from the seat, stepping clumsily
to the aisle, as Buzz, grinning heartily at the other grinning
passengers (who are actually relieved to see him and his
guitar moving away from them), strolls toward the empty
seats at the back.

I follow them, one or two of the others ahead of me—
between me and Cynthia—and one or two more sliding along
behind. We all sit around Buzz, presumably because he has
the guitar and it was his idea in the first place to come here
and sing. Cynthia is next to him, leaning towards him carefully, almost touching his beefy, sweatered shoulder with
her hamburger-bun breasts. Several young American skiers,
all of them looking like overfed Swedes, place themselves on
the wide end-seat on either side of Cynthia and Buzz. I am
draped over the back of the next to the last seat, staring
Buzz right in his blue eye and talking quietly all the while
to Cynthia: about order, the continuum, and the differences
between the two, about beginnings and endings, their absence
in our experience, about progression and the lack of progress.
All my obsessions. But Cynthia keeps her baby-blue eyes
fixed on Buzz's thick fingers as they do a stumbling imitation
of Carlos Montoya's.

Hey, swell! Here's a great one to start with! Buzz shouts,
beginning immediately to bang on the strings, crump, crump,
crump. Yeah! Everybody knows this one! He commences the
singing, with everyone (except me) joining by the second
word. We-shall-o-ver-cu-um! We-shall-o-ver-cu-um! We-shall-
o-ver-cum-sum-m-m-m-day!

And so on. I don't bother to keep time with head-
noddings now. At the right moment, I reach across the
space between Buzz and the back of my seat and grab his
bass-string just as he brings his hand down to crump all
six strings evenly, and I yank the string straight out, so
that his hand, rippling across the upper five, bangs into the
sixth and bounces back up, killing the song, naturally, and
probably hurting his hand, too. He stops, and everyone else
piles up on top of whomever he has been secretly following.
Except Cynthia, who seems to have been following a chorus
of singers not on this bus, who simply goes on singing, sweetly
and slightly off-key: We-shall-o-ver-cum-sum-day-ay-ay-ay . . . !
Deep-in-my-heart-I-know-that-we-shall-o-ver-cum-m-m-m-sum-
m-m-m (moving straight through to the finish now, all
alone, smiling, mouth wide open) day-y-y-y-y-y!

What did you do *that* for? Buzz barks at me.

Let th' broad sing, ya creep! Whaddaya, Melchior or

somethin', ya gotta drown th' broad out? *This* is what our hero came to see—not the "Christian Lady", not the happy songsters one and all, but the confused anger of the blond young man with the guitar. For he, the one called Buzz, he is the only one in the group, not counting F. B., whose mere thoughts can drown out the very voices of the others, whose pride is greater than all their vanities and whose guilt is greater than all their trivial shames. *He* is the one to be encountered, for he is the only one capable of, and thus driven to, the feat of swallowing up the others. F. B. included.

Lissen, mister, Buzz snarls, I don't know what kinda games you're playing, but I'm not innarested. Now, whyn't you just go on back down to the front of the bus and stop bothering people? he suggests, nipping angrily at the words with his even, perfectly white teeth.

I look to Cynthia, as if for understanding and pity. Securing assurances of same, I turn back to Buzz, who has much more understanding than Cynthia will ever have, but naturally, and as a direct result, no pity whatsoever. Look, I say to him, if this is some kinda closed group I'm breaking into, I mean, if this is some kinda *clique* or something and strangers belong elsewhere whenever you people get together to sing together, I'd be the last one to want to bust in and ruin the sanctity of the thing. (Outflanked him, though he probably saw it coming. Not the language, though. He never could've anticipated F. B.'s freedom from language, which is what allows *him* to employ *it*, rather than vice versa, even though Buzz probably possesses that very same freedom himself. Simply hasn't realized it yet, that's all.)

Just don't keep the rest of us from enjoying *our*selves, okay? We won't ask you to do anything you don't want to do, so long as you do the same for us. Okay? And right now, we want to sing. So if you can't join us and you want to keep on interrupting like you just did, we'll have to insist that you leave us. Okay?

Not okay.

What???

I said, *Not* okay.

Wal . . . well, then, you'll just have to take off, pal. Just move on outa here. That's all. G'wan, beat it!

C'mon, Buzz, forget it. He's just looking for trouble. Let's ignore him, huh?

Buzz glares the suggestion down, sends it flying back to its owner's original anonymity and silence with a wave of his thick hand. What are you after, mister? he asks, and I know it's all over for him now. He's too close to genuine curiosity and too far from direct challenge, and the only way he can ever get back will be if I decide to allow him back. Which, of course, I simply cannot do. Not now. He'll have to get back on his own now.

What am I after, Buzz? I'm glad you asked that question. Because *this* is what I'm after: I want you to take your guitar and march yourself right down to the front of the bus and request the driver to stop and let you off right now, or as soon as it's possible for him to do so safely. I smile benignly at him.

What??? You . . . you're out of your head! This is crazy! He looks to the others for confirmation, but they are looking to him for confirmation. Even Cynthia—whose pity has finally turned its light onto its real object, herself.

Do you think you can accomplish that, Buzz? I ask nicely.

Look, you're nuts! You don't know me, so I don't know what you're talking about!

I know you now, fella. Don't I? So let's hop to it. We're almost to Concord, the driver'll have to make a stop there, and you can catch a bus back to Boston in a few hours with no trouble at all. You'll even have time to take in a bit of the city. It's small, but it is the state capitol, you know. So pack up your guitar, Buzz, and get moving. Right now, fella! I add sharply.

Lissen, mister, *you're* the one who's going to get moving! he shouts, and he grabs my arm with one hand, his other hand moving quickly to assist his violence, and, consequently, letting go of the guitar's neck—a lost, hopeless, desperate move. For I simply grab the guitar by its neck where he had been clutching it, yank it down onto the floor next to my seat and stamp my foot through it, ruining the instrument with one blow. Buzz lets go of my arm, horrified, and falling back into his seat, he turns into a miserable, utterly miserable, young man staring down at his smashed guitar.

This is where you get off, I inform him, as we glide down Concord's main street.

The bus finally hisses to a stop before a small, cinder-block building which serves as a railroad station-taxi stand-bus depot. Buzz stands up weakly and moves slowly past me. You bastard, he says quietly. If I ever see you . . . if I ever catch you where I can deal with you . . . someplace like in a dark alleyway . . . I'll beat the living shit out of you!

Buzz! Cynthia exclaims, shocked. *Pity* him. He's a man we must all feel *sorry* for, not *hate*, she says. Please, Buzz. Stay. Don't get off the bus.

If I stay here, I'll kill the bastard!

Buzz! Cynthia cries, pitying him for his wrath.

You'd better get a move on, Buzz, I remind him.

I just hope you're happy, mister . . . 'cause if you set out to make me sick, don't worry, you did! And *that's* why I'm getting off this bus . . . because you make me sick! I'd stay if you'd leave . . . but you're not enough of a human being to do anything like that! No!

Don't beg me, Buzz. It's unbecoming. And it won't do you a bit of good. Not now.

You shit! he says, moving down the aisle for the door, grabbing his satchel from the luggage rack above his original seat at the front of the bus and his loden coat from the seat itself, then stalking glumly down the steps and out the door.

The remaining five or six at the back of the bus, including Cynthia, file past me in abject silence and return to their original seats, all of them, as they sit down, glancing out their windows at Buzz. Then, not understanding their embarrassment, their own senses of loss and secret joy, very quickly turning away.

A few miles down the road, with the bus passing through a small country village called Boscawen, New Hampshire, I walk forward and ask the driver to let me off as soon as he can safely do so. He is able to stop the bus after a few seconds in front of a barn-red general store. I pull my coat off the rack above Cynthia's head, drape it over my shoulders like a cape, and say good-bye to Cynthia. Take good care of yourself, baby, I sagely advise. And don't worry about ol' Buzz or me. You'll be wasting your time, 'cause we're both fine. You just do what comes natural, baby. Worry about Cynthia.

You gettin' off or not, buddy? the driver inquires.

Off, I say, and so I do.

Nobody looks out his window at me as the bus eases from the gravel parking lot to the road, heads north to the mountains.

Surrounded by head-high snowbanks, I began to hitch-hike back to Concord. The third car to pass me heading south, an old Ford station wagon driven by a tall, middle-aged woman in an army surplus field jacket, stopped.

. . . Home: Crawford, New Hampshire. Where one's parents reside.

There is snow on the ground, on the trees. Recently fallen, with no chance yet to melt from crotches and forks among the branches of the trees.

The house: squat, fat in the middle, and tapered at both ends where rooms, porches and garages have been tacked on over the years—haphazardly added and never quite able to merge with the main design of the house, even after decades. The house, its barn, the entire countryside—languishing warmly in late morning beneath the chill blanket of snow.

The dirt road, cleared by scraping off most of its snow cover, looking stark and brown, like dog shit, against the scrupulously white snow. Winds cross and finally flee the shadowed valley, dashing quickly along the road and disappearing in the north behind tall, slope-shouldered pine trees.

There are grey hills in the north beyond the pines. And huddled like sleeping bears beyond the hills, there are the White Mountains. The Presidential Range. There are lakes and rivers and streams; the tracks of glaciers everywhere. And the buildings seem almost as old as the land forms.

Among these buildings: the house. It sets back from the road about seventy-five feet. In the front yard, between the house and the road, loom two enormous elm trees. Crossing the yard, cutting between the two elms, a blue 1949 Ford panel truck, the chains on its rear wheels grabbing at the dead grass and frozen turf beneath the snow, yanking the truck backwards to the front door of the house, where it stops. Two men dressed in plaid wool mackinaws and caps

jump out of the truck, disappear into the house, and soon
return with armloads of articles from inside the house. Back
and forth, disappearing together into the house, then reappearing with their arms full, or at either end of some
huge piece of furniture or trunk, then disappearing into the
truck and coming out again empty-handed. Back and forth.
Back and forth. Their faces cannot be seen from where I
am (wherever *that* is, *wherever* that is). Only their broad
backs.

On the south side of the house there is a porch that
runs the depth of the structure. A man is sitting on the
porch. He rocks a rocking chair and peers off the porch to
the ground below, seeming to let his attention casually gather
the subtle details of the snow-covered meadow before him.
He is a heavy man, though not fat, and rather tall. He appears
to be in his middle twenties.

The two workmen busily carry furniture from the insides of the house to the insides of the truck. End tables,
lamps, cartons ostensibly filled with kitchen implements,
beds, mattresses, curtains, rugs, chairs, a sewing machine.
The small truck long ago should have been filled to over-
flowing, but still the men come and go with their arms full
of large, unwieldy objects, disappearing each time into the
back of the panel truck, like a long line of circus clowns disappearing into a tiny, scarlet automobile parked in the
middle of the center ring.

Finally, the two burly men come out of the truck for
the last time, and instead of returning to the house for more,
they step aside and face the open door, their backs against
the truck's open door, standing at attention, like footmen
for Cinderella. The man on the porch continues to rock and
look at the ground dropping away and spreading out like
water before him.

An old woman suddenly appears from inside the house.
She is tall and slender, with white hair tied up beneath a black
pillbox hat, and she is carrying a small, dark green steel
box and several large brown mailing envelopes. Deeds, con-
tracts, birth certificates. She walks purposefully out the door,
leaving it open behind her, and steps gracefully into the
rear of the truck. Then an old man appears at the door of the

house. He, too, is dressed in black. He is tall and thin, somewhat stooped, and his hawklike face is waxy with age. In his hands is a thick, mouldering, leather-bound bible—a Family Bible. The old man steps spryly away from the door and into the back of the truck, the footmen quickly closing the truck door as soon as he is inside. Then they walk around and get into the front seat of the truck, start the motor, and drive quickly across the yard, driving in their original set of tire tracks in the snow between the two elms, turning right when they reach the road (toward the south) and disappearing.

The man on the porch continues as before. The front door of the house is still open. This house is my parents' home. I am the man on the porch. (Look at his *face*, for God's sake, not to mention his posture!) I do not recognize the two men who have been removing all that the house contained. The woman, clearly, is my mother. Although I did not get a good look at her face. The old man was doubtless my father. They ignored me on the porch, all four of them. They behaved as if I weren't even there. I leap up from my rocking chair and rush into the cold, stripped house, to see if maybe they have accidentally left something useful or valuable hanging around somewhere. To see if *anything* has been left me. Anything at all!

THE DEFENSEMAN

For my father the idea of loneliness was early separated
from the idea of solitude, a condition imposed on him by
geography. Or it may be something he picked up from his
father. Regardless, it's a distinction that served him well.
Facing the threat of constant loneliness, it enabled him to
be literally fearless, and later on, when the pressure of
geography had been removed, it explained to him his continuing solitude.

He played hockey, of course. Like all Canadian boys,
even solitaries. A tough defenseman with great maneuver-
ability but not too much speed, he had the will, size and
ability, but especially the will, to break up a three-on-one
rush for the goal by rapping one kid with his stick (up
under the jaw, usually), taking out the second with a hard
check to the kidneys and the third by hurling his entire body
across the oncoming skater's path, slapping wildly with his
stick at the skittering puck, his back, slammed against the
third boy's rush, blocking any view of the puck, the goal
and the kid's own feet, bringing him finally crashing down
to the ice as at the same time his own stick discovered the
puck and punched it back to one of his grinning, slightly
embarrassed, slightly envious teammates.

Hockey, especially as played by Canadian schoolboys,
is a violent game. But the violence usually lies dormant
until the game is played by older, heavier, more motivated
and darkly competitive adolescents. Until then a boy's
violence is ordinarily a clumsy, harmless imitation of what
a man-sized player can do gracefully and with harm. Hundred-
pound kids skating like the wind, barking and yelling at each
other in French or Nova Scotia English, growling through red,

contorted faces, bumping theatrically against one another,
they only rarely (and then almost always by accident) enact
violence upon one another. For them the game, insofar as it
is violent, is pure theater, with themselves, their opponents,
their own friends and their opponents' friends, as audience.

Whether or not for my father it was merely an extreme
version of this theater, I couldn't say, but I do know that for
others his violence was real enough (I've been told by those
who knew him then) and that consequently he earned a
reputation as a hatchet-man on the ponds and public rinks of
Halifax before he was twelve, which is very unusual. Also,
until one is old enough to play in the tough, even brutal,
Junior League, such a reputation is useless, is possibly even
a liability.

To understand him, I try to recall how it was for me at
that age, because as a skater I had about the same ability
and lack of it that he had—maneuverable, with fast hands
and feet, large for my age, but not very fast and with a weak
slapshot no amount of solitary, early morning practice
could improve. I could never combine the hard charge for
the net with the sudden shot from fifteen feet that sent
the puck like a rifle slug about eight inches off the ice all
the way without once touching down past the goalie's dropping glove and lifting stick and into the net itself with a neat,
quick, kissing thud.

Like my father, I was a defenseman, and to increase my
value as a defenseman, I too relied on the will to extremity
that I knew the other players neither possessed themselves
nor expected to encounter in anyone else. Though we expected each other to imitate the older players, it was merely
to mimic their threats and gestures, the textures of their
violence. Consequently, anyone willing at that age to go all
the way, unhesitatingly checking, tripping, body-blocking,
rapping hands, heads and legs with his hockey stick, anyone
willing actually to *be* violent, had the considerable advantage
of surprise going for him.

Though I'm not sure why I should happen to seize onto
how as a child my father, or for that matter I myself, played
hockey, it is obvious that for a child raised in these north-

eastern United States and southern Canada, hockey and ice-skating in general are of surprising emotional significance, combining as they do, so early and for so long, social and private experience. Also, they provide an arena in which other people and an intense physical environment (ice) are positioned precisely to confront one's young and relatively untested, unknown body. As evidence of the staying power the experience holds, this past winter I've walked down to the pond in the meadow in front of my house perhaps no more than six times in all, and lacing on my skates, pushing off, gliding in slow, rhythmic ovals around the pond, alone and out of sight of the house, my mind backtracks in time, until before I am aware of it my physical responses (*to the glassine smoothness of the ice, a slight pinch of the toe in the left skate, ears, nose and chin crystallizing in the breeze caused by my body's swift movement through still, cold air . . .*) and the loose flow of my fantasies (*of suddenly breaking free of a tie-up at the boards, he's got the puck, he's going all the way in, the goalie's ready for him . . . and, Whap! a slapper, and the goal-tender goes down to his right for the puck, too late, and I SCORE! glide humbly, suddenly relaxed, past the net, shake loose clumps of ice-shavings from my blades, move like a gentle bear back down the ice towards my own goal and my teammates . . .*), at times like that, when I'm skating alone, my physical responses and my fantasies are coming straight out of childhood.

I've noticed in men from the midwest a certain, glazed, timeless look drifting over their faces whenever they're bouncing and heaving a basketball around and through a hoop tacked to the side of their own or a neighbor's garage. For southerners, at least the ones I have known, it happens around hound dogs, shotguns and rolling, tangled, half-cleared farmland in fall and early winter. I suspect at these times they're making the same, restful, return trip that I make when skating on the pond down in front of my house. Besides being a connection to one's childhood, a brief slip backwards into the consciousness of one's ordinarily objectified past, it's a connection with other men as well. Including my father, I suppose.

It's never really been clear to me whether or not for my
father the realities of ice and dream-like motion across its surface evoked images of family and origin, as they do for me.
I don't think my grandfather even knew how to skate, and
therefore I always assumed that my father (unlike myself,
for instance) had to learn to skate on his own, with boys from
the neighborhood. But because when I was a child we lived
far from anything even vaguely resembling a neighborhood, I
was allowed to learn to skate with my father, on Saturday
and Sunday afternoons the winter I turned six. It was an
event, formally announced as such. One Friday night my
father simply said, "This winter I'm going to put that boy
up on skates."

My mother clucked that I wasn't old enough. (I'm
piecing this together from bits of remembered conversation
and event, stories told later on, and what I know must have
been the case.) They were in the kitchen, after supper. My
mother was sitting at the table over the clutter of dishes,
resting a few moments before moving back to the sink again,
to clean up her kitchen and utensils one more time. She
was smoking a cigarette and drinking a cup of coffee. My
father was restless that night, was pacing, stopping occasionally to peer out the window into the frosty darkness. My
brother and I were playing on the floor like small dogs,
nipping and yipping, imagining tails. At the sound of my
name I stopped playing and sat attentively, a human again.
My brother, two years younger, went on barking and
growling.

The fire in the stove crackled softly, the kitchen was
close and warm, lit dimly by kerosene lanterns that filled
the room with a fluid, golden light darting and disintegrating
into flat planes of light and shadow as my father, huge in
the low-ceiling'd room, moved from window to door to
woodbox to black cookstove and back to the window again,
talking, as he moved, in a low, rumbling voice of his work,
how it had gone this week, the men he worked with and
for . . . his inestimable value. The air was filled with the odors
of hardwood chunks slowly burning, and food, Friday night
supper, fish, though we were not Catholic.

"This is a damned cold November, you know that? I bet
it hits zero tonight," my father announced.

My mother observed that at least there'd been no snow yet. She stubbed out her cigarette in the wet saucer.

"Um. The ice'll be perfect tomorrow . . . I haven't had my skates on in years," he said. "They're still up in the attic, aren't they? I remember hanging them on a nail up there two summers ago, when we unpacked."

"No one's touched them so they must be up there where you put them," she said.

He left the kitchen and in a few seconds could be heard clumping around overhead in the attic, looking for his skates.

In the morning, after breakfast, my father said to me, "C'mere, son, we're going to get you some ice skates and teach you how to use 'em." And with his to me enormous, blocky, leather and steel skates tied together by their thick laces and slung over his shoulder, he headed out the door to the barn to start the car.

Recalling her own freezing discomfort from some night years ago, the abject misery of the non-skater who must stand at the edge of the ice stamping heavy, numbed feet or else must skid in small, choppy circles on rubber soles, waiting like a cripple while the others glide gracefully past in long arcs that sweep them into the darkness at the far side of the pond, my mother tried to buffer me against the force of her remembered misery by wrapping me in heavy layers of wool and rubber clothing, until I was standing in the kitchen, stiff and immobile as a chair, red-raced and sweating. My father had backed the car out of the barn, idling, then racing the motor. He started rapping impatiently on the horn. My mother swung the door open for me, and I hurried out into the cold morning air, moving like a penguin.

The air was crystalline, almost absent. The fields lay like aged plates of bone, dry, scoured by the cold till barren of possibility, incapable even of decomposition. The trees, mostly pine and spruce in roadside woodlots, stood in the windless cold like blackbears crossly aching to sleep.

When we got to Maxfield's store in Pittsfield, my father peeled off several layers of the clothing my mother had laced onto me at the house, and I was able to move my arms somewhat and bend my legs at the knees. The skates were beautiful. Just like my father's but about one-quarter scale. They were stiff outside, as if carved from blocks of wood, yet when laced onto my feet, they felt like an old lady's gentle hands. Brown and black, hockey-style skates, the shoe was cut fairly low, except for the tendon guard at the back, and the blades, the lovely, steel strands that were going to lift me off the ice and free me from the yank of gravity, were toughly snubbed at the toe and heel. And sharp.

"Hollow-ground," the salesman assured my father, who tied the two skates together by their thick, yellow laces and draped them over my shoulder. I felt the sudden, surprising, downward tug of their weight.

Returning to the car, we got in and drove the half-mile or so to the east end of town, to Whites Pond, a small, shallow, man-made pond used in summer months as the town's municipal swimming pool, in the winter as a public skating rink. A log touching the shore, frozen where it had floated months ago, was the obvious place to sit and exchange shoes for skates. A dozen pairs of various-sized and -shaped shoes lay in the vicinity of the log, and out on the ice a couple of men and a crowd of boys were slapping a puck erratically back and forth in furious, structureless sport. It was early and they had been on the ice only a short time and were merely testing themselves, each other and their equipment before choosing sides for a game.

My father pulled my shoes off and replaced them with my new skates and laced them up for me, asking me, when he had finished, if I thought I could do it for myself from now on, telling me that I must remember to lace them each time all the way from the toe. "And *tight*, son, as tight as you can get them. That's lesson number one," he said seriously.

Then he put his own skates on, stepped gingerly from the bank to the ice. As if he had suddenly taken flight, he was gone.

Standing, my weight wobbled on the short thin lines that the blades had become, and then my ankles gave way, and I tipped and fell on the ground behind the log, wondering what had happened. I could not see my father anywhere.

Deciding that the ice would make the difference and

that once on it I too would stand and fly off with incredible, weightless grace, I dragged my body like a bundle of sticks and cloth down to the log, over it and out onto the surface of the pond. Once again I stood up. Then I waited for it to happen, for the beautiful speed to come.

But in seconds my body, seeking balance from some point in space high above the blades (diminished by now to paper-thin sheetmetal), overcompensated and tipped, pitching me to the ice, where I remained for some time, utterly bewildered, my ears reddening with shame. My vision was rapidly narrowing, closing in on me, and now I was afraid that I *would* see my father, would see him scornfully watching me.

Again and again I struggled with my body and lifted it to a position that roughly approximated a standing position, and before I had a chance to locate it relative to the bank and log behind me and the vast expanse of ice in front of me, it was lying facedown again, arms and legs splayed, as if thrown to the ice from a great height.

Eventually, knees and elbows aching, the base of my spine feeling like a star of pain, I was able to hold my body in a standing position for what seemed like hours. Slowly, carefully, I raised my eyes from my feet, trusting them finally not to betray me, and saw that I had traveled halfway across the pond. The shore looked like a horizon. Not twenty feet away from me a crowd of men and large boys were viciously slashing at the ice with hockey sticks. They surged back and forth, like a dogfight in water, skate blades slashing and stabbing, ravening teeth against the ice.

Then suddenly they were gone, racing away in raucous pursuit of the tiny, black, fleeing puck. Their legs and shoulders seemed to move only from side to side. It was as if the skaters were casually bouncing off the opposite banks of a narrow stream in the middle of a large flat field— and yet they flowed smoothly away from me. Attempting to imitate that powerful side-to-side motion, I pushed off my right skate and toppled over like a stack of bricks.

This went on for a long time, until I discovered that I could move, slowly, clumsily and with great pain, in a forward direction. The cold, from my having lain on the ice so often and for so long, had crept through my coat, sweater and flannel shirt, and I was shivering. The small of my back and my neck had contracted into hard knots of ice that were beginning to spread quickly through the rest of my body. I ached everywhere, and my ankles felt like thick drums of gum rubber.

I was heading painfully back towards the bank, sliding single step by sliding single step. I imagined that I was pushing off my skate blades from one side to the other and was cruising across the boney surface of the ice at an incredible speed, when suddenly my father swept out of nowhere, like a moving waterfall, slicing hugely across in front of me, careening powerfully over to my other side. Where he changed direction! Skated *backwards*! And I saw then that I was plodding, step by painful step, at about one-eighth my normal walking rate.

My father grinned and nodded and said, "*Good, good. You're doing fine, son. Real fine.*"

But I knew that I wasn't.

The ride home, about seven miles, seemed to take mere seconds. My father and I talked almost not at all, which, normal for us, seemed especially so that day. My mind was filled with a new sense of my body, a sense that while it may well have been made of some kind of malleable substance, it nonetheless possessed a shrewd, persistantly willful and possibly cruel mind of its own.

I did not see the trees and fields as we passed, did not even notice that we were home, until my father, having shut off the motor and opened his door, said to me, "You coming in or going to sit there till dark?" I jumped, but then I saw that he was smiling easily.

As soon as we were inside the house my mother rushed to me and I quickly showed her my skates and claimed confidently that I had learned how to ice skate. My father did not contradict me. Taking off our coats, he and I stood together near the stove for a few minutes, warming our hands and feet, and when I asked him if we could go skating again soon, he said, "Tomorrow, if you want."

I said that I wanted to, right after breakfast, and he

grinned at me with appreciation and then at my mother with triumph, and that's the end of the story of how my father taught me to ice skate.

Trying to remember if I've ever seen any pictures, snap-shots, of my father and me that show us skating together, I realize that none of the pictures that have come down to me from those years show us, any of us, in the winter. The wintertime snapshots inevitably are of the house banked in with headhigh snowdrifts, the dates and descriptive comments always written on the back by my mother.
Jan. 12th, 1943! Wow! The big one! Doubtless taken to impress our cousins living in regions to the south of us, a way to brag of our hardiness.
Our house, March 21st, 1946! First day of spring! Ha-ha! Just the house, or maybe nothing more than the fluff-crowned roof and tops of the windows barely visible above the snow. There are never any people to be seen. My mother and my brother and I must be inside the house, looking out of one of those dark, small-paned windows at my father, as he stands out by the road, snow up to his waist. Holding the box camera squarely in front of his belt buckle, he squints down into the viewfinder, finds the view sufficiently desolate, and snaps the picture.
Probably it's simply that the cameras most people owned in those days were not very effective in the dim, grey light of winter. But even so, it is odd that fully one-half of our yearly existence then is represented by less than a dozen pictures of our house and automobile, when the other half of the year seems to have been photographed endlessly.
Another curious aspect of this is that, even though my conscious memories of those years are almost completely of summertime, it was the winter that dominated our activities, filling our talk and views of the rest of the world (so that we could not even speak of a place without first mentioning that it enjoyed a climate that was kinder than ours). Of events that took place in summer, however, I recall only the general condition and have obtained my formal knowledge of the events themselves solely as data. It's as if they could as easily have occurred in someone else's life.

The conditions surrounding an event, the textures, physically, emotionally, spiritually, these remain uniquely our own; the particulars of an event, what we use to name it for strangers, are no more ours than our dates of birth. Perhaps this is why so much of the act of remembering is an act of the body, and why, sitting in my livingroom late at night, I can recall none of the particular, isolate experiences that, inevitably, come swiftly back to me in a solid, complete block when, at the end of a November day, I grab my ice skates off the nail in the barn, walk across the road and cross down through the grey butts of winter-grass to the pond. The sky is like a peach-colored sheet drawn taut at the horizon, a high rim miles away that circles the center of the pond. The air is still, thin and cold. In a week there will be a thick pelt of snow over everything that today stands before me like grey, brown and lavender bone, cleaned and scoured by cold alone, neither dead nor dormant, but fixed, held in time the way a snapshot freezes a gesture at its completion. And as long as the fading daylight holds, the pond, black and smooth as a gigantic camera lense, is the precise center of the sphere of space into which I have placed myself. I cannot see the house or the road from here, can see no way out.

I sit on the steep, rock-hard, eastern bank and take off my boots and put on my skates, and when I stand up, I am on the ice, moving across the pond's black surface like a man running slowly through a dream, on a level plane, but also inside a matrix, as if underwater, free of gravity's grating tug but free as well to ply my body's weight gracefully against it, like a dancer sliding against the felt measures of time.

SEARCHING FOR SURVIVORS (II)

It was early afternoon in the west, in the east early evening. Reed had been unable to sleep for more than a few jumpy minutes of the six-hour trip. Capable of sustaining only occasional and haphazard, momentary ruminations, he couldn't even focus his attention sufficiently to read the magazines that the stewardesses had persisted in shoving in his face nor follow the bouncing progress of the Barbra Streisand movie they had projected onto a little screen two seats in front of him. He was exhausted and still a bit drunk, his body's rhythms broken and scattered. His stomach was churning angrily, and his head had begun to ache. Whatever comfort he felt came from the sodden kind of relaxation that flows from a sense of having finished a dirty job, and when finally he gave up trying to divert himself, had resigned himself to immersing thought passively in his body's vague and general discomfort, the plane began its descent into Boston.

The ground below, in semi-darkness, was greyly sheeted over with old snow, except for the black crescent of the harbor and the city clinging to its outer edge. Moving pinpoints and tiny squares of light speckled roads and dark blocks of buildings—suburban towns ringing the city of Boston, and Boston itself. The plane circled out over the bay, passed over whitened islands and occasional beacons swinging hazy arms, dropped again, completing the circle, and headed for the airport from the east across water, landing smoothly with a huge, long roar of wind and jet engines, and finally taxied to a stop and silence before the glass walls of the terminal.

Reed stood up and pulled his coat down from the shelf, grabbed his briefcase and made for the exit. Hurriedly, as he descended the ramp, he jammed his arms into his trenchcoat

and buttoned it around him, shoving his free hand deep into
the pocket, automatically groping for car keys. He found
them—where he'd dropped them two weeks earlier. He felt
also something that at first was unfamiliar to his touch—a
piece of cloth. A small, coarse, slightly stiff piece of fabric.
He fingered it idly, walking to the terminal gate, and once
inside, drew his hand out of his coat pocket, bringing with it
the piece of cloth. Striding quickly up the carpeted incline,
he rounded the first corner and saw beside him a waist-high,
white plastic, rubbish receptacle, and he dropped into it the
torn and filthy, light-green half of a man's sock that was in
his hand.

He rubbed his hand against his coat and walked quickly
away, following the white and blue signs to the baggage dock.
He kept his thoughts directed ahead of him, aiming his mind
like a flashlight, shining it only on the seventy-five mile
drive north to home, wife waiting in the kitchen, expecting
him for a late supper, two daughters watching television, up
past the usual bedtime because of the occasion, house warm
and brightly lit, filled to brimming with affection, pleasure,
relief, etc., for his having returned home safely. Nothing
but clean, conventional images from the life of a young
family that treasures its own continued existence.

Morning. A few additional inches of snow had fallen
while they'd slept. Reed woke late, around ten, shaved and
dressed—heavy twill trousers and a flannel shirt—and came
downstairs, still tired, as if his body weighed twice its normal
weight.

The smell of fresh, hot coffee and bacon and eggs cooking
helped. As did his wife's face, smoothly smiling at him as he
sat down at the kitchen table. He knew that she was deliberately contriving a perfect, moderate gaity, and he was grateful for the contrivance. The real thing would have repelled
him.

"Your father called while you were sleeping," she said
casually, pouring coffee into a mug. "I told him you'd gotten
in late last night all worn out and would be sleeping late."

"Thanks."

"I told him you'd be in touch with him first thing."

"First thing." He said the words slowly, with reluctance acknowledging to himself that the job was not finished yet, nope, would not be finished until he had told the whole story over again, from start to finish, to his father, and then to his father's mother and sisters, and doubtless to all the East Coast members of his mother's family too. He was beginning to doubt if the job would be finished even then. Or ever.

"Well," he said, "I suppose I have to go over there and see him today."

"No way you can do it by phone?"

"Not really. No. Besides, my mother gave me some pictures of Allen that she wanted him to have. I promised her I'd see that he got them. It's got to be done, I guess." He could already feel his cheeks freezing into the phoney smile that he shoved his face into whenever he had to be with his father, even though, he realized, no smiles, phoney or otherwise, would be required today. What would be in order today would be a passive grimness, an expression which showed that one must take death in stride in this walk through life, that one must accept the good with the bad, the bad with the good, and that the cliché that only the good die young, while true, all too true, was, through some riduculous inversion, absolution rather than condemnation.

"What'll you tell him?"

"I guess I'll just have to tell him what happened. What else is there?"

"He'll want some kind of reassuring, you know. When someone dies . . . especially when it's your child . . . there's always a big bag of guilt to be dealt with. And in your father's case, the guilt will be monumental," she added.

"I know, I know," Reed said brusquely, scraping his chair back and getting up from the table.

Around eleven, he left his house in Crawford and headed for his father's house in Piwacket, forty-five miles across the state, in the direction of Vermont. The road had been freshly plowed and salted and looked like the long, curling tongue of some mythic, white beast. He drove between high snowbanks across the rolling countryside, through tiny villages and past old farms, nineteenth century colonials and Capes with barns attached by sheds stacked to the rafters

with firewood, farms now used mostly to house the grandparents of the people who lived in the suburbs of the city,
or younger people, like Reed, whose income didn't depend
on the land, or like his father, whose small construction business could be sustained by the state's stable, though deflated
and rural, economy. Over the river, the Merrimack, and
through the woods, New Hampshire's, to Papa's house he
went.

———————————————————————————————

   From the east, arriving like the sun, he comes swiftly
with silver wings upon his feet. Nearing his destination, he
begins to hear, and then even to see, wailing women shrouded
in black. They step slowly from behind tall palm trees when
he passes down the long, wide avenue, and they stand behind
him, keening as the sun sets red in the Pacific, a burning,
waxen ball sinking into the sea. In the grey-green light of
early evening, with the thick odor of tropical flowers drifting over dew-wet ground, he arrives finally at his mother's
home, a white, stucco'd building where elderly, solitary
men and women live in small apartments that face onto a
square, grassy courtyard. Bronze sprinkler heads poke
through the grass, ominous and treacherous in the dark, like
grenades. The courtyard is empty as he approaches, doors
closing silently seconds ahead of his glance, blinds drawn
quickly, stealthily, across the windows as he passes by.
Porch lights go off, one by one, until there is but one light
left shining, the one above the door at the northwest corner
of the courtyard. He walks, a saddened prince in a foreign
kingdom, along the narrow pavement. Then turns to his
left, nears the door with the light above it. And as he steps
up to the door, it opens suddenly in front of him. Without
hesitation, he moves into the dim room, and the door closes
behind him.
   Several people are inside the room, waiting in the shad-
ows among the furniture, standing as he enters, holding half-
filled glasses in their hands. The only face he sees is his
mother's face, rushing towards him, her small, down-slashed
mouth open, shaped like a crescent moon, points reaching
downward to the horizon, eyes red and streaming tears
across cheeks, blond-dyed, short hair wildly storming about

her head, hands stretched out in front of her, grabbing at
him, his shoulders and face, his own hands, which he releases
from her grasp by pulling her shuddering, small body to
him and stroking her slowly on the back and the moist back
of her head, crooning quietly to her in a low, steady voice,
until she begins to hear him, and her cries gradually subside,
so that she can hear him saying, "No, no, now, he's not
dead, we don't know that he's dead yet, so try to be calm,
we'll find him, don't you worry now, it's all right, he's all
right, he's all right now, don't you worry now, we'll find
him, it's all right now, I'm here now. . . ."

Over her shoulder and behind her in the gloom of the
apartment, he sees the face of his lost brother. A photograph in a brass frame set on a maple buffet against the far
wall. Next to it, also in brass frames, three other high school
graduation photographs—of himself, his other brother
Preston, and his sister May. He cannot see those three faces
smiling eagerly at him across the room, can see only the
most recently made photograph, probably taken sometime
in the last month—a large face as full and as broad as his
own, with a mouth like the mother's, dark eyes like the
father's. A witty, yet serious, expression has been caught
flickering across the smooth face. It watches the older
brother casually, stabbing him in awful, detached cruelty
with a knife of self-consciousness, forcing Reed to watch
himself console his hysterical, wailing mother as if he were
watching a film of it. He yanks his gaze away from the
photograph, looks into the distraught face of the woman
who still clings desperately to him, sees that it's too late.

Outside South Station, he parks his car illegally on
Summer Street, trusting that his out-of-state number plates
will keep the car from being towed away by the Boston
police. The day is warm and clear, even here in the city, with
a fresh breeze blowing the soot and exhaust up from the
streets and out to sea. He strolls into the huge, cavernous
building, an almost deserted hall, the walls covered with
advertisements and political posters. Remembering how it
was when he was a child, crowded with travelers waiting for
trains to leave or arrive, servicemen in uniform, students re-

turning to school or drifting back to their parents' houses on
Long Island, families headed for New York or Chicago or the
far West Coast, even, for holidays or just to travel there, businessmen, salesmen, Boy Scout troops, groups of just-arrived
foreign students or shopkeepers on tour, and above the
noise of the shouts and talk and babies' bawling, there was
always the hollow, monotonous, authoritative voice announc-
ing the arrival and departure of the trains, a chanted accomp-
animent to the noise of the hundreds of travelers caught together momentarily inside a single building in a city—and
remembering this, he crosses the nearly deserted, silent hall,
walks in a straight line towards the one open ticket seller's cage,
crossing empty space where once there had been rows and
rows of wooden benches, and he begins to wonder if he has
made a mistake, if he's come to the wrong railroad station.
Is this place even *used* anymore? No, the letter had said
distinctly, *South Station.* Underlined. Allen wouldn't have
made a mistake like that. Not he. If there was one thing
that kid would have got right the first time, it would be
where his train came in, and when. Besides, he would've had
to change trains in New York, taking the New York Central
to Boston, and South Station is the only place in Boston
where trains arrive from points south and west. So this must
be the right station. He'll be here at 12:15. Just as he said
in his letter.

Reed checks his watch. 11:45.

The narrow-faced man inside the ticket seller's cage
finally looks up, peers through the bars at him, says, "Yeah?"
His skin is thin and waxy, a yellowish pink color. A small,
breaking wave of white hair rims the top of his smooth head.

"When's the next train from New York?"

"One-fifteen." He goes back to counting, wets his thumb
with the flicking tip of his tongue.

"One-fifteen?"

He looks up again, slowly. "Yeah." Back to counting.

"Isn't there a train comes in from New York at *twelve-*
fifteen?"

Once again, the man looks slowly up, his face this time
tightening with annoyance. "I said *one-fifteen.* That's the
next one. Now, anything else? You want a schedule?" He

reaches across his counter and flops a white folder in front
of Reed.

"Chicago. When's the next train from Chicago?

"Three-forty. Wanta try Providence?"

"No. No, thanks. I guess there's been a mistake. Sorry."

Reed walks slowly across the hall to the gates and strolls
along the row of numbered, frosted-glass doors, past occasional, fifty to sixty year old men in blue denim shirts and
floppy dungarees, men he assumes work for the railroad.
Switchmen and yardmen, brakemen possibly. Featherbedders?
he wonders. They stand and lean against the half-open doors,
looking out at the tracks and talking quietly with each other.
Most of them carry black lunchboxes. They pause in their
conversations and look at Reed with idle curiosity as he
passes. For a moment he wonders why, then remembers
that he is dressed in paint-spattered levis, shirt and boots
and probably has spots of white paint on his face, too. House-
painting, he wants to tell them, to answer their questions.
They probably think I'm an artist, he decides. What will
Allen think? He hasn't seen me in . . . seven years? No, five.
When he came east five years ago with Ma to visit us in North
Carolina, he was twelve, just a twelve year old kid then, kind
of chubby and nervous. But unusually gentle, especially
with little children. Most kids that age don't even notice
babies or two year olds unless they accidentally step on
them. But he was eager to hold his nieces . . . no, his niece.
Sadie wasn't born then . . . talking to her gently, sweetly,
until he had her following him around the house like a puppy.
And Ma, to us, as if Allen weren't near enough to hear her:
"*Look*, look at Allen with her, so *sweet*, what a *sweet* boy!"
And he'd say, "Ah, Ma!" and grimacing in pain, he'd put the
baby down and walk heavily off to another part of the yard.
"I know I shouldn't talk like that in front of him, it em-
barrasses him, but isn't he a *sweet* boy? He's just like *you*
were, Reed. You must see that. Why, when he was a baby,
you'd hold *him* like that, talking funny to him, making all
those crazy faces of yours. It's the same age difference, you
know," she said, as if discovering suddenly that she were a
distant relative of a person famous in history. "*Eleven years*!
Allen was my change-of-life baby, he *was* unexpected, you

know," she said to her son and daughter-in-law, her voice dropping to a more confidential level. "I don't know, maybe I really *did* want to get pregnant and just didn't know it or something. It's possible, you know. We were pretty careful, but sometimes when your marriage is on the rocks you think you can save it if you're pregnant. He had always been so good and all involved and everything when I was pregnant with you three. But not *this* time. No *sir*. He was working away from home all the time then, coming home only on weekends every other week, and of course drinking *very* heavy. Allen was just over a year old when his father left us," she sighed. Then pouring herself another glass of beer from the brown quart bottle beside her, she adjusted the angle of the chaise and lay back down in the sun, closing her wild eyes behind white-rimmed sunglasses.

Five years ago. North Carolina. Allen will be different this time, but so will he, Reed, be different. Older by five difficult years, beginning already to grey at the temples, like his mother at thirty. His face is aging even faster than hers did and, because it's not from drinking, differently from his father's. He wonders how he will seem to his brother now. Almost thirty years old. That will separate him from a seventeen year old kid by an entire generation, he calculates, and as he turns at the far end of the row of numbered gates and begins the walk back, he decides that he will try to stay loose this summer while Allen is living with him, will try to act a few years younger, will not be so careful and deliberate and will try to hold onto the odd bits of information that he usually discards and forgets because they seem to him useless to anyone over the age of twenty-one. And at the same time he will make it easier for Allen to act older than he's able to act when at home with his mother.

At twelve-fifteen, a train departs for Providence. Less than a dozen passengers board it, mostly older men in dark suits who look like retired railroad workers—ex-conductors and tickettakers. The chain of seven or eight maroon, soot-covered coaches glides slowly away, lumbering gracefully from side to side, the electric diesel engine making a steadily increasing growl that, in the distance, melts into the noise of the wheels against the rails. Why on earth would a kid raised

in southern California be hung up on *trains*? Reed wonders,
remembering their telephone conversation last winter, when
he first made the offer to Allen, saying to him, "I'll send you
a roundtrip ticket from LA to Logan Airport in Boston, in
early June, okay?" thinking it would be a glamorous offer
to a boy who had never flown before. He had assumed that
their earlier trip east, the one to North Carolina, had been
by train only because of the need to save money, so he was
astonished when Allen had answered, "No, whyn't you wait
till I find out what the cost is for a roundtrip train ticket,
and then send me a check instead?"

"*Train*? You mean, *railroad* train? From Los Angeles?
And back?"

"Yeh."

"You don't want to *fly*?"

"Not especially. Besides, do you know what the accident
rate is for airplanes, as against rail travel?" he asked his
brother.

"No."

"Well, according to the National Safety Council, there
were zero-point-seven deaths per one hundred million miles
of rail travel last year. That's way below the per mile rate of
air travel—zero-point-three-eight per hundred million miles—
and especially when you consider that so much of rail travel
is short distance hauling, which means that the number of
passengers per hundred million miles is way higher for trains
than for airplanes," he said. "Check it out," he advised cooly.

"I'll take your word for it."

But if he can be so exact about the death-figures, why
can't he be exact about when his train gets to Boston? Reed
wonders, slightly annoyed. Strolling out to Summer Street
to make sure that his car is still there, he spots the green
Volkswagen bus, and relieved, confident now that it won't
be towed, he walks back into the cathedral-like interior space
of the station. The entry, a short arching corridor, is an
arcade between windows of shops that once displayed racks
of gaudy gifts for generous travelers, windows now boarded
up with unpainted sheets of plywood. The hall smells slightly
of urine mixed with the smell of shoe polish, though the
shoeshine boys have been gone for a decade. He checks his

watch again. 12:25. The clock high on the wall, an enormous
brass ring with Roman numerals bolted to brown, speckled
marble, indicates with long, thin arms an hour that doen't
exist—the minute-hand points directly at XII, while the hour-
hand is stuck halfway between X and XI. It's exactly ten-and-
a-half o'clock, he thinks.

At the newsstand, a solitary island in the middle of the
hall's sea of space, he picks up and pays for a copy of the
Boston *Globe* and walks to the only other concession in the
station that's open for business, a coffee shop—a counter with
a dozen plastic-covered stools, a short, gum-chewing blond
leaning on her fists and dreaming of riding in a convertible
to a lake in a summer night with her hair blowing behind
her like a palomino's mane. Reed orders a cup of coffee from
her, and when he's read through the newspaper, he folds it
up and looks at his watch again. *One-fifteen*! He pays for
his coffee and starts running for the gate, where he'd noticed
earlier a sign that said New York City, glancing over his
shoulder at the clock on the wall while running, as if for
confirmation. It still says ten-and-a-half o'clock. His boots
clack loudly against the filthy marble floor. When he reaches
the now-opened gate, he can see that the train has already
come in. Oh shit! What if we've missed each other, after all
this! Ten or twelve scattered passengers are walking earnestly
towards him. A batch of middle-aged businessmen in rumpled
suits and carrying briefcases. A woman vaguely resembling
Pat Nixon in a white knit suit and pillbox hat stuck to the
top of her head. A tall, bearded man with black, Germanic
cameras dangling from his neck, banging against his chest and
medicine-ball stomach. Then he sees Allen, coming last,
shambling along with a bear-like gait, wearing a field jacket
over flapping dungarees and tee shirt, long, brown hair drifting over ears and across broad forehead, big grin spreading
over his face when he spots Reed waiting at the gate. He
shifts his duffle bag to his left hand and sticks out his right,
which Reed grabs onto and pumps.

The two walk rapidly across the station towards the
exit, Allen filling the air between them with talk of his
journey east, talk that's exclusively of trains casually referred
to by number, of the differences between lines, Southern

Pacific, Penn Central, Canadian Pacific, the Long Island Line, Seaboard, even the old Boston and Maine, of costs and profits and losses and tonnage and mileage, with statistics and figures dropping off his lips as easily as the names of popular singers and athletes. His knowledge is encyclopedic, his interest obsessive, his delight total. He is amazing, and Reed, amazed, shakes his head with happy disbelief. The two pass out of the station onto Summer Street, and Reed looks at the empty place where his car was.

"Do you know what has just happened to me?" he asks his brother, interrupting the monologue.

"Huh? No. What?"

Starting to laugh, he tells his brother what has been done with his car, and they walk to the corner of Summer Street and Atlantic Avenue and climb into a cab.

"We had a memorial service for him," I was telling my father. "We *had* to, as I told you when I called you from LA. For her. To give her something concrete . . . to frame whatever comes afterwards. You know. And, of course, we had to because there was no body. The flowers you sent were fine. Very lovely, a huge arrangement of yellow roses. She was very grateful," I went on, relating as concisely as I could the facts that, I supposed, more or less told the story for him. There was so much else that I wanted to tell, information that, while not exactly factual, was no less information for that. Impossible, though. I would only have confused him, then frightened and finally antagonized him. So I went on, describing the brief, simple ceremony we had arranged, leaving out of my story completely the one small event that clung to my mind and probably will remain there long after the rest has been forgotten.

My sister May and Gerry, her husband, and my brother Preston had gone on to the church ahead of my mother and me. They were supposed to arrive before any of the twenty or so of Allen's friends, to "greet" them (as the minister had put it), Press and my brother-in-law to escort them to seats down at the front of the church, close to the center aisle, so it wouldn't look like such a small and eccentric gathering. My mother and I were to leave for the church late, so that

we could be the last to arrive and enter. A section of the
pew in front would be reserved for the five members of the
family. The others, whom we had invited to the service on
a basis of close or longtime friendships with Allen—with a
few exceptions for a couple of my mother's closest friends,
without whose low-voiced consolations and advice, she kept
insisting, she never would have got through this—these others,
we assumed, would all be seated by the time my mother and
I arrived. This was thought to be something of a necessity,
because of the probability that, if she were to come face-to-
face with several of the people we had asked to be there,
boys who had shared Allen's obsession with trains and had
therefore been his most intimate friends for years and the
one or two adults who in one way or another had tried to
help the attractive, bright and essentially fatherless boy, the
intensity of such a confrontation would be too great for her
to bear. She was exhausted, and in spite of tranquilizers and
two arduous weeks of our constantly shoring up her controls
against hysteria, it was clear that she was still about to be
flooded by a total, screaming hysteria that we had no con-
fidence could be ended. We were terrified.

When it seemed time, I walked my mother out of my
sister's apartment, where she had been staying since Allen's
disappearance, to the car I had rented, and the two of us
slowly drove the couple of miles across town to the church,
a brick Congregational church that was not more than five
years old. "It was *our* church, you know, so I'm glad we're
having the service there, I mean, not because it's a *Congregational* church or anything, but because the minister, a
wonderful man, isn't he a wonderful man, don't you like
him, he told me I'd meet lots of *very* fine people there,
lots of New Englanders go there, you know, we New
Englanders come out here to California and we've *got* to
have our Congregational church, just like at home . . .," she
chattered as we drove. I let her ramble, nudging her back to
harmless topics whenever I saw that she was drifting too
close to words that, before she knew it, would slam her up
against the wall of Allen's death and break her like a glass
jar. Easing up to it, even touching that wall with fluttering
fingertips, measuring its limitless height and length, was

something she could manage, but only when she had prepared herself and could move slowly and deliberately forward to it and then quickly back again to where she did not have to see it for a while. I told her what we were planning. Some music, a very short sermon with no lingering morbidities, some more music, and then home. And I told her again who would be there. She was glad for all of it. "Just right," she said. "That'll be just right. Just right."

We drove into the parking lot, large enough for a shopping center, I thought, and I parked the car as close as I could to where we would exit from the church. "How do I look?" she asked me, the voice of a daughter suddenly afraid of her own wedding asking her father how she looked. "Do I look all right?"

"Fine. You look lovely." She was wearing a high-backed, black chintz dress and long, black gloves, and a small, round, black hat with a veil that covered her eyes. She had put on too much makeup, and tears had already smeared her eyes into black smudges that in moments would be charred pathways down her cheeks. Her lipsticked mouth trembled, and she lit a cigarette. "Let me sit here a minute and try to get a hold of myself, all right?" she asked me. "It's all right if I smoke?"

"Sure."

She sucked the smoke deep into her lungs, inhaling several times, and after a few more drags, stubbed it out in the ashtray. The stub had a ring of lipstick around the filter tip.

"Ready?"

"Yes. Just don't let go of my arm, okay?" she asked.

"Don't you worry. I'll keep hold of you till I get you back to May's," I promised.

We got out of the car and very slowly walked to the front portico of the church, a concrete slab with three square, red brick columns rising from it to a triangular-shaped roof overhead. I had hoped that no one but Press, May and Gerry would be waiting for us there, but obviously some who had come to mourn had also come to console. A small crowd of adults and tall, gangly, uncomfortable-looking boys were waiting for us as we stepped up to the entryway.

The first to come forth and touch my mother was a tall, bald, dark-eyed man with a short, black moustache. He looked like the publicity director for a chain of resort hotels. Taking my mother's gloved hand in his huge, hairy one, he held it and looked ponderously down into her tiny, birdlike face. "Eleanor, we are all soo-o-o sorry . . . , " he began in a sleek voice, which she swiftly interrupted by turning around to me, placing his hand into mine, and saying brightly, "This is Judge Pfizer, you know, you've heard us talk about Allen's friend the Judge." And to the Judge: "This is my oldest son, Reed, I know you've heard us talk about *him*!"

The Judge and I shook hands gravely, and he passed into the nave of the church. Then came two ancient ladies with faces like parchment, swiftly passed on to me and intro-- duced as Mrs. Nordine and Mrs. Baugh, who for years had lived in the same apartment house as had my mother and Allen. They probably managed to take in upwards of ten funerals a month. Then I was introduced to a cat-faced musical director from Allen's high school, and the slender, whiskey-voice, middle-aged widow from down the street whose kitchen-sized lawn Allen had mowed once a week for the last year.

The others remaining, a couple of paunchy fathers and their teen-aged sons, had started to go in as soon as the Judge had spoken for them—doubtless what he'd intended, whom he'd meant by "we"—but suddenly my mother, letting go of my arm, ran to the last person to go into the church, grabbed his elbow and spun him around to face her, astonished. He was a tall boy, well over six feet three, and thin, with long, curly, brown hair flowing over his collar. She reached up and threw her arms around his neck, pulling his head down to her, and kissed him full on the mouth, then released him. Clutching both his enormous hands in her small, puffy ones, she said quietly to him, "Danny, thank God *you* came. If *you* hadn't been here, the whole thing would have been wrong." She smiled up at him and he backed uneasily away from her. Ignoring his discomfort, she waved her hand at him, a small, floppy wave. He waved back, turned and quickly went into the church.

Walking slowly back to me, still smiling, she took my arm again and said, "Well, should we go in now?"

I said yes. Moving towards the door, I asked her who that boy was.

"That's Danny Perry," she said brightly. Then, more confidentially: "He was the boy at Berkeley that Allen was going up to visit when the train wrecked. Danny'd been writing letters all fall to Allen, just *begging* him to come up there for a weekend, and I knew how awful this must be for him, so I wanted to let him know that now I love him more, not less. I should think that would be important to him, don't you?" she asked, looking up at me, sincerely, for an answer.

"Yes," I said. And then I saw Press standing next to me, staring at his mother's face. I placed her arm into the crook of his, and my sister and her husband and I followed them into the darkness of the church.

It was almost noon when Reed got to Piwacket, a village on the Contoocook River comprised of a block of wood frame storefronts, a dozen large, white houses, three filling stations and a now unused covered bridge that crossed the river ten feet downriver from and parallel to the road. He drove through the town, crossed the river on the new metal and concrete bridge and turned left at the fork where an A & P was being built. He drove down the road for about a quarter of a mile, through a stand of new pine, black-green branches drooping with the weight of snow, and at the end of the pine grove turned right, into a driveway, and parked the car in front of a closed barn door. A large red sign nailed to the barn door said *Carter's Construction Co. / General Contractors/ Piwacket, N.H.*

Reed got out of his car and walked across the squeaking snow to the side porch of the house, stamped his feet on the porch, getting rid of the snow from the driveway that had stuck to the warm bottoms of his boots. The door opened in front of him, and Georgia, his father's third wife, smiled and invited him in.

"Hello, Reed," she said to him in her low voice, as he passed by and walked into the kitchen. "Good to see you again."

"Thanks. How're you?" Around fifty years old, she seemed much younger, unless you looked closely and saw

the hardened creases around her eyes and mouth, the tiny
purple veins spreading across her cheeks and forehead. She
was a vain woman and obviously worked hard to keep herself attractive to men like Reed's father. She was slender and
had a good figure, pouty breasts and smooth, well-shaped
legs and a narrow waist that she emphasized by wearing
shirtwaist dresses with buttondown collars. She tinted her
hair, keeping it shiny black, and wore it short with studied
casualness. For Reed the most attractive thing about her
were her jade green eyes, deep green and set wide in her face,
catlike. Reed, when he had first met her five years ago, right
after his father had married her, had tried to find something
about her that he enjoyed seeing, and he had settled on her
eyes. Thus, he was able to be polite and indifferently friendly
when he had to see her, which almost always was the case
whenever he had to see his father. She worked as his secre-
tary and bookkeeper, and the office was an extension of the
kitchen. "Is my father here?" Reed asked her.

"Sure is," she said smartly. "Sam! Reed's here!" she
called, cupping her orange lipsticked mouth with her hand,
as if it were a great distance from the entrance of the kitchen
to the office and drafting room just beyond. Sam liked to be
called, Reed knew, didn't like Reed to think he had been
waiting eagerly to see him. Also, it was one of the numerous
ways in which he tried to convince his son that, though he
was a harried, successful businessman, he was never too busy
to take a few minutes out for family.

He came into the kitchen, drafting pencil stuck behind
his ear, hand stretched out to Reed, face fixed carefully in
an expression that mingled equally pleasure at seeing his
son and sadness for what he knew his son had come to
tell him about. He was wearing chinos and a plaid, wool
shirt and a dark grey, wool necktie, a fairly tall man, the
same height as Reed, but heavier, thicker. He carried half
again as much bulk as Reed did, bearing him down, so he
usually slumped to a few inches shorter than Reed. He had
a genuine presence, however, a physical intensity that allowed
him to center a room, like a potter centering a chunk of clay
on a wheel, as soon as he entered it. His once black hair was
almost completely grey, was thin and receded sharply at his

temples. He combed it now the same way he had combed it as an adolescent in the nineteen-thirties—straight back and without a part. Because of an extremely large face, his head seemed larger than it was, and thus it was often impossible, even for people who knew him well, to recognize him from behind. Obviously, as a young man he had been quite handsome—large, though well-proportioned structure, dark, deep-set eyes, a straight, long nose, full mouth and well-shaped chin—but alcoholism was beginning to take a toll. His nose was permanently swollen now, and veined and pocked, and the texture of his skin was that of an unhealthy man, as if it were being dried and salted from inside. His eyes were seldom clear, even when he was sober.

They shook hands somberly, and Sam motioned for his son to sit down at the table. "Georgia," he said, "can you make us some coffee?" He lit a cigarette, inhaling the smoke through his nostrils.

"Shoo-wah," she answered, an exaggeration of a Yankee accent that she used whenever possible, probably believing that it contributed to an image of perky, youthful energy.

"Have you had lunch?" Sam asked his son.

"I had a large breakfast late. But you go ahead and eat lunch if you're hungry. I'll be happy with a cup of coffee."

"No, that's all right. We'll eat later," he said. He's covering himself with unusual grace today, Reed thought. The limits for our visit are set perfectly now—one hour at the most, and then I leave, and no one feels slighted.

Reed lay the manilla envelope on the table in front of him and opened it, pulling out the photographs. "My mother . . . Eleanor . . . gave me these, except for two of them." (Still, after all these years, he wasn't sure of how to refer to his own mother when talking to his father. When with her, he always referred to his father as "the old man" and never hesitated or felt embarrassed for it. But when the situation was reversed, he stumbled over his names for her— "my mother", "Ma", "Mom", "Eleanor", and once he'd even said, "your wife . . . I mean, ex-wife.") "They're pictures of Allen. His high school graduation pictures . . . he would've been graduating this June." He pushed an eight-by-ten and a wallet-sized print of the same photograph across the table to his father, who took them up and studied them carefully in silence. "She said Allen had been planning to send them to you."

Sam held the pictures in front of his face, staring at them both, switching his gaze from one to the other, from the almost life-sized portrait to the miniature, as if they were of two different people whose supposed resemblance he was trying to determine for himself. Georgia looked over his shoulder at the pictures. "*Handsome* boy," she pronounced.

"He really had grown up," Sam said slowly. He was seeing his son for the first time since the divorce, sixteen years ago. There had been no visits, no letters, no exchange of photographs, no vacation snapshots. Nothing between them at all. Not even last summer, when for most of three months Allen had been living and working forty-five miles away from his father. "The way I see it, if the kids want anything to do with me, they'll come to me, just as you did," Sam had once explained to Reed.

Georgia brought the coffee, instant coffee, watery, and Reed started talking, talking steadily, as if delivering a prepared speech, narrating the series of events in precise, chronological order, from the first phone call from May saying that Allen had supposedly hopped a freight to San Francisco to visit a friend at Berkeley but he hadn't shown up there and the train he had planned to ride had been wrecked in a mud slide north of Santa Barbara—to his return home last night. His father didn't once interrupt the narration, simply sat there staring at the photographs of the dead boy.

Reed was through talking before he'd expected to be. I guess it's a simple enough story when you tell it that way, he thought. Why does it seem so complicated and as long as a novel whenever I think of it beforehand?

"Oh, I almost forgot," he said. "Here are two more pictures, not very good ones . . . They're Polaroid snapshots taken of the wreck before the bulldozers moved in, after they got the fire out. I didn't take them, I got them off the one helpful official I met out there, a guy in the Santa Barbara sheriff-coroner's office." He handed over two fading snapshots of the wrecked train, taken from the highway embankment above the washed-out and harrowed railbed. One had been taken from the north end, near the engine, the other from the south, where the caboose had been. Except for the three sections of the diesel engine, which had flopped over intact on their sides, the train resembled a collapsed skyscraper—rubble, twisted, torn steel, collapsed and sundered compartments, scorched ground plowed violently over scrub brush and grassy shoulders on both sides of where the railbed had been. If the two graduation pictures had provided evidence that the boy had lived into his adolescence, these two snapshots proved that he had died.

Sam stared at the two pictures of the wrecked train, showing no emotion on his face, then passed them back to his son. "Well," he sighed, "I lost him twice."

It's late, long after midnight. The others, Gerry and May, have gone to bed, but she can't sleep again, and my rhythms out here are nocturnal anyhow, so I'm staying up with her. I'm saddened by the idea of her sitting here in my sister's livingroom, watching the Johnnie Carson Show and old movies on television, downing beer after beer at a rapid pace, trying to thicken her jiggling nerves with alcohol until she's able finally to sleep for a few hours, and the idea of her doing that alone is simply too pathetic for me to allow it—though I would love to leave now, to get into my rented car and drive out to the beach and drink in a bar for a few hours. The fine, objectified noise of a crowd of strangers, after so much of my own voice saying things I can't recognize, might help bring me back to some secure sense of myself. . . .

But there'll be time and plenty of occasion for that in a few days. Tomorrow I'll be six hours in a plane, alone, and surely that'll do me as much good as drinking in a beach-side bar three thousand miles from anything that vaguely resembles home. . . .

So I decide to sit here this last night with my mother, doing it as much for May and Gerry, I suppose, as for her. Press did the same thing for me last night, his last night here before going home to Portland. So few chances, now that we've successfully scattered ourselves across the country, for

us to offer these small generosities to each other. That's
pathetic too. And pathetic that we three surviving children,
we survivors, loved Allen only in secret and never had the
pleasure or gave the pleasure of uttering it full-faced to him.
Pathetic that his death didn't free us to do for each other
now what we'd been unable to do for him then. Press, this
afternoon at the airport, going home to his wife in Portland,
shakes my hand like a business associate trying to convey
unfelt sincerity, and I am unable to do more than respond
in kind. The same, safe distance between me and May and
Press. Even though all three of us know now‑ if ever we
hadn't known it before—that each of us, just like Allen,
will die momentarily. Mother too. In a minute, we're all
going to die, killed by some unexpected, huge, speeding
block of steel, BANG! Caught in the middle of a thought
or sentence. Gone, absolutely gone, and the survivors will
never have another chance to make us understand anything.
What's been said up to this moment by Press to me and me
to him may just be the sum total of all that can ever be
said between us. I can't believe that we have been so stupid,
so incredibly stupid and weak, that we go on doing it! Good-
bye, Press, give my best to your little wife up there in fine,
woodsy, old Oregon. Have a pleasant flight home. Don't
die, old fellow! And tomorrow, to May and to Mother, I'll
give a kiss and a wave, a few cheering, last-minute promises
and vague assurances, and I'm off. So long, folks! Like
Woody Woodpecker at the end of the cartoon, "That's all,
folks!" You've got it all, every bit. But no, that's just it, you
haven't got it all, every bit. You haven't even got one-
hundreth of what I feel about you, what I could say if I
were able to know with my body what I know with the
front part of my brain—that I am going to die, and you are
going to die, and one of us is probably going to die momentarily. . . .

My mother is startled by my question. I've never asked
it before, in all these years since the divorce. "Did I *love*
your father, love him enough to tell him so? You mean,
just like that, I *love* you?" She's sitting up straight in her
chair, smiling at me on the couch, her chin pulled in tight,
like a goose making a difficult decision. She holds her glass

of beer out in the air in front of her, six inches or so off her lap, a cigarette in the other hand tightly held between tobacco-stained fingers.

I nod yes, that's what I mean, just like that, I love *you*.

"Well," she says, taking a deep drag on her cigarette, "of *course* I told him. *Lots* of times. Especially when we were first married, we were very much in love and so we were always telling each other that we loved each other."

"What about later?"

"Well, I used to tell him, because he really didn't believe it. He was always accusing me of . . . he was an extremely jealous man, *you* know that, so I used to tell him a lot that I really did love him and he really didn't have to worry about me, and it was the truth too. Towards the end, of course, it didn't make much sense to say it, even though it still was true."

"What about him? Was he able to tell you that he loved *you* ? I mean, so that you could believe it and know that he wasn't just trying to please or flatter you or anything like that. What I guess I'm asking is, were you and he able to make each other believe that you loved each other? I know you worked hard at convincing him, but I wonder if you succeeded. You follow me?"

"Certainly, Reed, of course I follow you. Well, now, about whether or not I ever convinced him . . . well, I honestly don't think it was possible for him to believe that I or anyone else ever loved him. Even when he was a boy Allen's age. That's how old he was when we first started going out together, you know. But even then he was always suspicious and cynical. I'd have to go someplace with my family and couldn't go out with him and nothing I could say would convince him that I hadn't gone out with another boy. Nothing. Sometimes I think that's why he was always so good with you kids when you were little babies and then just seemed to ignore you as soon as you were old enough to talk. When you were babies he knew he didn't have to be suspicious of you. But he just could not believe that any person half-grown could love him. It was his mother and father who did it to him, you know. She spoiled him rotten and his father would turn around and beat him black

and blue. They used him to settle their differences with each
other, he once told me, and I can sure believe it. Even when
he was a seventeen year old boy in high school—no, he'd
already graduated by then, he was so smart, you know, he
graduated from high school when he was only fifteen, but
dumb me, it took me till I was nineteen but of course I was
sick for a year. Anyhow I can remember him with welts
and bruises all over his body, from where his father had
beat him for practically nothing. It's no wonder he didn't
trust anybody. I remember the very first date we had, I
practically had to ask him out. He was, you know . . . not
interested in girls, I mean, not that he liked *boys*, oh no, he
just didn't want to ask any girls out that he thought would
turn him down, so until me the only girls he went around
with were cheap tramps. You know. Anyhow I had seen
him at school, we were both working in the senior play, I
can remember it as clear as yesterday, *The Man Who Came
to Dinner*, it was. And Sonny Tufts, you know, the famous
actor? He had the lead and I had the second female lead,
and he was the one all the girls were after. But he had asked
me to go to the cast party with him. His name wasn't Sonny
then, of course, it was Bowen. Bowen Charleston Tufts. A
huge boy with beautiful, blond hair, silvery blond. He played
on the football team, a star, and he had a beautiful singing
voice, you wouldn't believe it. Well, Bowen had asked me to
the cast party but I had been watching your father, Sam, he
wasn't *in* the play but he worked on it, I think he built the
sets or something. He was only fifteen then, and very handsome, everybody thought so, but he was supposed to be
kind of wild, you know. He ran with a fast crowd. Ernie
Thompson, Mike Kelly, a bunch of wild guys who drank
very heavily and spent a lot of time with girls they picked
up in Boston. But I liked him an awful lot anyhow and I
thought he liked me. He had talked to me quite a bit when
I was so nervous about remembering my lines, showed me
some tricks to help me remember certain hard lines that
I kept forgetting. So when Sonny Tufts, Bowen, asked me
to go with him to the cast party, I said no because I hoped
and thought your father Sam would ask me. But he didn't.
The day of the party, the same day of the play, came nearer

and nearer and everyone else had their dates and Bowen had
asked another girl and still Sam wouldn't ask me. Right up
to the night of the play which was really a great success
because Sonny Tufts was such a talented actor, even then.
So the night of the play just before the curtain went up I
was standing in the wing waiting to go out and take my
place on stage and up walked Sam and he asked me, 'Do
you want me to cue your lines from offstage, just in case?'
Well that was like a voice from heaven to me at that moment
because I was terrified, terrified of forgetting my lines. So
I threw my arms around him and kissed him and I said to
him, 'Sam, please take me to the cast party after the play?'
And he said he would. Just like that. 'Sure,' he said. Later
on he admitted that he would have asked me right at the
beginning but he was sure I would have turned him down
so he didn't. But if I hadn't asked him myself he never would
have asked me himself. Never. We wouldn't have seen much
of each other after that and he and I would have graduated
that June even though I'm older than he is and that would
have been the end of it, the end of our ever knowing each
other at all. So it's a good thing I said something to him,
isn't it? I mean, because he never would have said anything
to me. Not him."

I agree with her, and she goes on talking, now telling me
stories I've heard dozens of times. Always, the first story
she tells me is the only one I won't already have heard before. Interrupting her in the middle of the How-I-Found-
Out-Sam-Was-Cheating-on-Me tale, I take her empty glass
out to the kitchen, and opening a new quart of beer, refill it,
making a scotch and water for myself. She hears the ice
clinking all the way from the living room and asks me to
fix her a scotch too. "No. You're on tranquilizers, remember?
It's bad enough you're drinking beer, for Christ's sake," I
add.

She admits that I'm right, assuring me that she wouldn't
even drink the beer if she could stand the stronger tranquilizers but all they do is confuse her without providing tran-
quility. I deliver the glass of beer to her and sit down on the
couch again, my feet on the coffee table. My mother's
attention has wandered back to the television screen, so I

try following with my own. It's an old film. I wish it were a
Sonny Tufts film. But it's not, it's an Italian spectacular,
about blood-lusting Vikings. The dubbing job is an inept one,
and the actors' lips snarl and chew angrily against the words
we hear. I look over at my mother, to see if she's managed
to coordinate the speeches with the speakers, but she's asleep
in her chair, slumped off to one side, one arm dangling limply
over the endtable, her chin tucked against her chest.

Getting up from the couch, I snap off the TV, and then,
after spreading the blankets that my sister left folded at the
end of the couch, I touch my mother's shoulder lightly, and
when her eyes flutter, I say, "C'mon, lady, time to close this
place for the night." She nods agreement and struggles to her
feet, and I help her to the couch.

She's still sitting there, in the middle of the couch,
staring through half-open eyes at the blank, wide-open eye
of the television screen, as I say once more, "Now lie down
and go to sleep," and go out the door to my car, to drive to
the far side of the city to the apartment where she has lived
for eleven years with her son Allen.

Reed's green microbus, going from his house in Cata-
mount to Concord, the state capitol. A twenty mile drive.
Early September, the trees and grass looking parched, the
deep green pine trees greyed over and drooping thirstily,
the leaves of the hardwood trees slightly yellowed. Fields
of brown hay. Farm ponds down, rimmed by dried mud
aureoles. White clapboarded houses standing out against
the drab background with a clarity of color, texture and
form seen often in the midwestern states, rarely here.

Inside the box-shaped vehicle, Reed driving, his brother
Allen in the passenger's seat next to him. Allen fooling
with the radio. Smoking a cigarette. Staring absently out
the window. Fooling with the radio again. Reed just driving,
saying little, receiving short answers from Allen.

To Concord. A city of less than thirty thousand people,
most of the businesses facing a long, wide Main Street. State
office buildings and gold-domed capital building at one end,
small industrial plants at the other, the whole town resting
on a shelf of glacial sediment overlooking the meandering

channel of the Merrimack River. The microbus goes slowly down Main Street, heading south. Turns left at the traffic light in the exact center of town, goes down Pleasant Street to the Greyhound bus terminal, a small, square cinderblock building at the end of a block of recently built stores. Reed parks the car in the lot behind the depot, and the two get out, Allen pulling a large, very heavy duffle bag from the back, slinging it over his shoulder. They walk into the depot. After a moment they come back outside and sit down together on a wooden bench next to the door.

Reed, looking at his watch: "These buses are usually right on time coming down from White River Junction. I don't think we'll have to wait more than five minutes . . . You'll be in Boston by eleven-thirty easily."

Allen, popping a stick of chewing gum into his mouth, chomping down on it as he speaks: "You're sure I'll have time to get from the bus station down there to South Station?"

Reed: "What time's the train leave?"

Allen: "One, exactly."

Reed: "No trouble at all. The bus goes to Park Square. You just walk out to the street and get a cab, there are always plenty of them hovering around the bus station. It's only a five minute ride to South Station from there."

Allen: "Good."

Reed: "You sure you got enough cash on you?"

Allen: "Oh, yeah, no problem."

Reed: "Can you use a couple extra tens?" Reaches for his wallet.

Allen: "Well . . . actually, just in case. If I miss my connection in Chicago, I might have to stay over for a day."

Reed, pulling two ten dollar bills from his wallet, folding them in half, handing them to his brother: "Here . . . just in case."

Allen, shoving the money into the right front pocket of his levis: "Thanks a lot."

They sit silently for a few minutes, watching the cars pass. Allen lights and smokes another cigarette. Flips the butt with his thumb and forefinger into the middle of the street when he's finished.

Reed: "Listen, be sure to tell everyone out there that we send our love."

Allen: "Right."

Reed: "And I hope you have a good year this year, you know, an improvement over last year . . . with school and all. And remember, about college? I meant what I said, you can go ahead and count on my helping you. Just get yourself accepted . . . anywhere, it doesn't matter . . . and I'll make sure your tuition and the rest of it somehow get paid. I'll back you up, kid. Naturally, you should try to get whatever you can from the college first, scholarships, I mean."

Allen: "Scholarships! Shit, I'll be lucky to get into a country branch of U-C, with my grades." Spits into the gutter.

Reed: "What about the junior college right there at home? They have to accept graduates of the local high school, don't they? I mean, you can always transfer later on."

Allen: "Yeah, but I won't go to school and live at home with Ma. This is the last year I live at home. Period. No matter what. Even if I have to let them draft me into the army."

Reed: "Well . . . at least keep my offer in mind, just in case. Okay?"

Allen: "Right. Thanks."

Reed: "I gotta take a piss. Be right back."

He gets up from the bench, walks into the bus station and disappears into the men's room. After a few minutes, he comes back out and sees the bus from White River Junction has arrived. Its flat, silver side fills the plate glass window of the depot, blocking out practically all light. Through the glass, he can see Allen talking to the uniformed driver, helping him shove the heavy duffle into the opened luggage compartment on the side of the enormous vehicle. Reed walks quickly outside.

Reed, raising his voice to be heard over the noise of the bus: "Well, listen, kid, have a damned good time going home!"

Allen: "Will do!"

They shake hands, quickly, and then Allen walks around to the front of the bus, climbs up the steps into it. He takes a seat halfway down, on the side facing Reed. His large face grins down through the dark, green-tinted glass, as if he were underwater. He waves casually. Reed waves back. The driver shuts the door, clunks the bus into gear, releases the air brake, and starts the vehicle moving away. Slowly back up Pleasant Street, second gear, catching the light, turning left onto Main Street, and then gone from sight.

Reed, standing alone in front of the bus depot. Walking slowly around back of the building to his car. Sitting in his car for a few minutes, looking at his hands. Starting the motor. Driving home.

Reed and his father. Shaking hands slowly, seriously. Reed standing on the porch, his father just inside the kitchen, the door between them wide open. Georgia out of sight behind Sam, the noise of cups and saucers being washed in the sink. Sam holding onto a large and a small photograph with his left hand, while he shakes his son's hand with his right. He wears a blue mechanical drafting pencil up behind his ear. Reed has his coat on, is standing slightly sideways, his left shoulder aimed off the porch, towards his car parked in the freshly plowed driveway. Sam's shoulder is aimed into the kitchen, towards his office in back of it. It is as if each man were trying to pull the other away from where he would like to go, Reed to his car, Sam to his office.

Finally, they let go of each other's hand and take a single step back from the threshold.

Reed: "Well, Pa, drop by the house next time you get over to our part of the state."

Sam: "Will do. And you come by here anytime, I'm usually working in the office these winter days, you know . . . . And bring the kids, too."

Reed: "Will do."

Sam, after a second of silence: "How's everything with the agency? You're still with them, I take it?"

Reed: "Oh, sure. Everything's fine . . . though I've got two weeks' work piled up on my desk, waiting for me to get to it." Shakes his head in mock disgust. Smiles. The busy life of a bureaucrat.

Sam: "Well, take it easy."

Reed: "Right. You too."

Georgia calls goodbye from the sink, Reed answers.
Waves a hand at his father. Gets into his car. Hears his father
closing the kitchen door solidly behind him.

I left home for good when I was seventeen. As it was for
my brother Allen, it was impossible for me to go to college
then without living at home—and the idea of living at home
for four more years was as unthinkable to me at seventeen as
a decade later it was to Allen. The pressures placed on her
children by my mother's sustained hysteria and dependence
were sufficient to bring them to a point, usually in late
adolescence, where they had to choose between staying
at her side and hating her for it, or loving her from afar. In
either case, the guilt was mind-boggling. But regardless, the
choice was a necessary one for all four of us. I chose to
leave. As did my brother Press, two years later when he
joined the Air Force. May decided to stay, and even after
she got married, she felt compelled to live in the same town
as her mother. Allen, however, having watched the suffer-
ings of his sister, was about to follow the example set by
Press and me.
I left in the morning, about an hour before sunrise. It
was in 1958, and I told my mother, and everyone else, that
I was going to Cuba, to help Castro win his war for Cuban
independence. In reality I had no idea where I was going.
Just away. We were living then in a large, industrial suburb
of Boston, in the top floor apartment of a shabby, five-
storey tenement house. She got up with me when my alarm
went off at five and while I dressed made me a large breakfast of bacon and fried eggs. We talked quietly while I ate,
mostly of whether or not I would be able to keep in close
touch with her from Cuba. I decided not, but promised to
do everything within my power to get letters to her as often
as possible. And, I reminded her, there was always the
chance that I'd be unable to make the contacts in Miami
that would get me over to Cuba. In which case, I would
just get a job in Florida and wait for a contact to show up.
And, too, there was the chance that the war would have
been won by the time I got down to Florida. The way things
were going—Castro was already at the outskirts of Havana—
this seemed more a likelihood than possibility.

Then, from down on the street, I heard the horn of the
car that had come to pick me up. I would be traveling with a
friend who was a Marine stationed in North Carolina, a tough-
minded, quick-witted, Italian kid a year older than I and a
year ahead of me in high school. While home on leave he had
purchased a new, white, Chevrolet convertible. The plan was
for me to ride down to North Carolina with him, then to
hitchhike the rest of the way to Miami. I looked out the
livingroom window and down to the street. Ah, he had the
top down.

Turning around in the darkness of the room, I reached
out and hugged my mother tightly, telling her not to worry,
that I'd be all right. She said she couldn't help it, she just
couldn't help it, she would worry, no matter what. She
kissed me on the lips and I felt the wetness of her cheeks
with my dry cheeks and knew that tears were streaming
over her face like nervous hands. "Go ahead," she told me,
"or he'll leave without you." I snatched up my duffle bag
and ran.

Outside, down the rickety, wooden steps of the porch
to the street, throwing my duffle into the back seat of the
car, jumping into the front, punching the driver excitedly on
the arm—and then he gunned the motor, popped the clutch,
and we were off. The cool, summer dawn air rapped against
my face as we sped down the turnpike, the sky behind us
slowly turning from deep lavender to pink, to a light shade
of peach, and then gold, with silver-edged clouds scudding
for the dark, western horizon, as if pulled by a magnet.

No body was ever found. The wreck burned for a day
and a half, and then the bulldozers arrived, wheezing, grunt-
ing, shoveling away and half-burying the twisted steel and
charred remains of thirty-five railroad cars, half of which had
been carrying new Plymouths stacked three tiers high on
each carrier. The bulldozers worked all night, once the fire
was out, clearing the devastated railbed away as quickly as
possible, treating the wreckage of the train itself as garbage,
useless rubble, pushing it off the railroad company's right-
of-way onto hummocky acreage that belonged to the state of
California. The urgency, to reestablish the crushed stone
railbed and to lay new tiles and rails, was so that the normal

flow of freight traffic between Los Angeles and San Francisco could be quickly resumed.

Reed arrived the day after the fire had stopped, the
morning the bulldozers finished interring the remains of the
train. He was with his brother-in-law Gerry. They parked the
car at the side of the highway, got out and walked along the
low guardrail, looking down the muddy embankment to the
gang of workmen spreading conical piles of blue crushed
stone with their shovels. The men worked rapidly, in unison,
swinging shovels easily and cheerfully. The rain had finally
broken, after almost a solid month of it, and the sky was a
deep, washed shade of blue. Everything dripped water—trees,
bushes, rocks, buildings, cars.

"Go ahead an' poke around it you want to," the foreman of the work crew told them. "We looked through everything already with a fine-toothed comb, once the fire was out.
Before we brought the dozers in. Sometimes there's a hobo
or kids on the train and we don't realize it, ya know, so we
gotta check, just in case, whenever something like this
happens," he said off-handedly. "But we didn't find nothing
this time. 'Course, if he did what you say, your brother?
hopped it in the yard down in LA, wal, he might've been
able to get inside one a them cars on the car-carriers. Sometimes they accidentally leave one or two unlocked after they
get 'em loaded, an' if they do, nine times outa ten anyone
hoppin' the train will try the car-carriers first. An' it was
rainin' that night too, and these guys ridin' the rails, ya
know, they like to get into one a them nice new cars an'
outa the rain. So he probably woulda tried the cars first.
Then, I dunno, maybe the middle caboose. But only if all
the cars were locked, like they're *supposed* to be anyhow,
an' also assumin' the kid was even *on* the train in the first
place. An' you say you don't have any real *proof* of that, do
you?" He looked at the two young men with heavy-lidded
condescension, drew a cigarillo out of his shirt pocket and
lit it, taking short quick puffs.

"Well, we've got enough information so that *we* know
he was on the train when it wrecked," Reed said.

The man shrugged, not caring. "Mister, if you wanta poke
around down there for a while, go ahead. Anything happens,

it's your responsibility. There's still lotsa odds 'n' ends down
there that're sharp as hell, so you cut or break anything, it's
your own responsibility. Far as I know, you sneaked down
there on your own. Nobody's supposed to be here that
doesn't have written permission from Southern Pacific anyhow." He stuck his hands into his trousers pockets and
stomped off, stepping over the guardrail a few yards down
from them, then side-stepping his way down the embankment to where his men were replacing the destroyed railbed.

Reed and Gerry moved a few yards in the opposite
direction, crossed the guardrail and, following the foreman's
example, side-stepped carefully down the mucky slope to
the wide ditch below. They said nothing as they descended
and were breathing hard when they got to the bottom. Reed
took off his trenchcoat and folded it across his arm, and the
two crossed over the ditch and climbed up the bank opposite,
to the roiling acres of bulldozed wreckage—huge slabs of
steel, violently shattered structures of wood and metal, all
of it blackened and blistered from the fire, and all of it driven
brutally into the bottomless mud.

It was hopeless. Reed stood on the bank in front of the
wreckage, his face limp and grey, hands at his sides, coat now
slung over his shoulder. "Gerry, there's nothing ever going to
be found here," he said in a low voice.

Gerry came slowly up and stood beside him, his round,
blond head nodding agreement. He finally said, "Yeah, but
listen, let's just walk over the site, once. If we find anything
in this mess, anything at all, it'll be because it was fate, you
know? Let's give fate a chance to work, okay? I mean, shit,
you never know. Right?" His open, sincere face looked im-
ploringly into Reed's. "If you don't do this, you'll probably
spend the rest of your life wondering what you might have
found."

Reed agreed, apologizing. The carnage of the scene was
total, absolute, so that he could not visualize how anything
not made of steel could have avoided complete destruction.
My brother wasn't just killed here, he decided. He was destroyed. Decimated, and then incinerated. Poof. Gone.

They found, upside down, the tops buried, three of the
fifteen automobile carriers. Then, scrambling over the under-

side of one, they saw the middle caboose, wheels gone, but otherwise still basically intact. It had been gutted completely by fire, and the bottom, once timbers eight inches thick, was a heap of charred fragments. The cage-like doors at both ends were locked with padlocks which had partially melted and fused with the clasps. The glass was gone from one of the end windows, so Reed climbed through the open square and dropped into the moist, burnt gloom of the interior. Water dripped from the roof, as if from the roof of a cave. He stumbled across rubble and huge rocks that were shoving up through the floor's charred remains, making his way with difficulty to the other end of the car. There he saw that somehow one corner of the car had escaped burning. The wood of the flooring and the painted steel wall, unlike the rest of the interior, hadn't been scorched and blistered back to the raw metal. It was an area in the corner, a few feet high and three feet along each wall, and in the corner, where all the lines of the car's floor and two walls came to a point, lay a small crumpled piece of green cloth. Reed reached down and plucked it with his hand, as if it were a flower, and stared at it. It was part of a man's sock, the part that covered the foot from the instep to the toes. The material and the color of the sock were the same as the material and color of the half-dozen old pair of socks Reed had given to Allen last summer, work socks, because Allen had come east with nothing but fancy black dress socks. They were U. S. Army surplus, and Allen had been delighted by the gift.

He shoved the piece of cloth into his coat pocket, then worked his way back to the window and clambered out to the open air.

"Anything in there?" Gerry called to him from a pile of twisted steel girders about fifty yards away. He was standing on the end of one of the girders, a few feet off the ground, bouncing on it and lifting slightly a mangled heap of steel at the other end.

"No. Nothing. The doors were locked anyhow. He couldn't have got into the middle caboose if he'd tried to." Reed walked over to where Gerry continued bouncing idly, climbed up onto the girder and joined him there. Their combined weights accomplished no more than the weight of one alone, just succeeded in joggling the pile of rubble at the other end.

"C'mon, let's get out of here," Reed said. He suddenly felt like a fool, standing in the middle of the devastated site, joggling a steel lever against tons of wreckage, as if it had something to do with his brother's death or the search for his body. "He's gone. Looking for him here is ridiculous," he said. "He was here, but he's gone now. That's all we need to know."

They went back down the near side of the ditch, crossed the new railbed and climbed slowly back up the embankment to the road. Gerry went around the car and got into the driver's seat, Reed slid into the passenger's seat. As the car pulled into the whizzing traffic of the freeway, Reed looked out the open window at the torn, muddy plain below. It looked like a place where a war had been lost.

ABOUT THE AUTHOR

Russell Banks was raised in New Hampshire and eastern Massachusetts until 1958 when he left New England to attend (briefly) Colgate University and to work as a shoe salesman, librarian, plumber, truckdriver, department store buyer of fabrics and draperies, moviehouse manager and dishwasher in numerous towns and cities of America. He attended The University of North Carolina at Chapel Hill from 1964 to 1967 and after graduating returned to New Hampshire where he now resides with his wife and three daughters. With the poet William Matthews he founded and co-edited *Lillabulero* magazine and press. His poems, stories, articles and reviews have appeared in many magazines and anthologies. *Snow,* a book-length poem, was published in 1974, and *Family Life,* a novel, in 1975. At present he is writing a second novel and teaching at The University of New Hampshire.

FICTION COLLECTIVE

Books in print: